LOVER BOY

"Look!" said Pleskit urgently. *"Look!"*

Tim turned around. Linnsy Vanderhof, his upstairs neighbor, was walking toward them. He shrugged. "What's the big deal? I see Linnsy every day."

"Are you so blind to beauty?" cried Pleskit. "Is your soul so dead to poetry on the hoof?"

Tim turned back. He stared at his friend in concern. "Are you okay, Pleskit?"

"Out of my way!" ordered Pleskit. Pushing past Tim, he puckered his lips and raced toward Linnsy, crying, "Kiss me, baby, *kiss me!*"

Books by Bruce Coville

The A.I. Gang Trilogy
  Operation Sherlock
  Robot Trouble
  Forever Begins Tomorrow

Bruce Coville's Alien Adventures
  Aliens Ate My Homework
  I Left My Sneakers in Dimension X
  The Search for Snout
  Aliens Stole My Body

Camp Haunted Hills
  How I Survived My Summer Vacation
  Some of My Best Friends Are Monsters
  The Dinosaur that Followed Me Home

I Was a Sixth Grade Alien
  I Was a Sixth Grade Alien
  The Attack of the Two-Inch Teacher
  I Lost My Grandfather's Brain
  Peanut Butter Lover Boy

Magic Shop Books
  Jennifer Murdley's Toad
  Jeremy Thatcher, Dragon Hatcher
  The Monster's Ring
  The Skull of Truth

My Teacher Books
  My Teacher Is an Alien
  My Teacher Fried My Brains
  My Teacher Glows in the Dark
  My Teacher Flunked the Planet

BRUCE COVILLE

PEANUT BUTTER
LOVER BOY

Illustrated by Tony Sansevero

A MINSTREL® BOOK

Published by POCKET BOOKS
New York   London   Toronto   Sydney   Singapore

This book is a work of fiction. Names, characters, places and incidents are products of the author's imagination or are used fictitiously. Any resemblance to actual events or locales or persons living or dead is entirely coincidental.

A MINSTREL PAPERBACK *Original*

A Minstrel Book published by
POCKET BOOKS, a division of Simon & Schuster Inc.
1230 Avenue of the Americas, New York, NY 10020

© 1999 Fox Family Properties, Inc.
Fox Family and the Family Channel name and logo are the respective trademarks of Fox and I.F.E., Inc. All Rights Reserved.

Text copyright © 2000 by Bruce Coville
Illustrations copyright © 2000 by Tony Sansevero

ISBN: 0-671-02653-4

First Minstrel Books printing January 2000

10 9 8 7 6 5 4 3 2 1

A MINSTREL BOOK and colophon are registered trademarks of Simon & Schuster Inc.

YTV is a registered trademark of YTV Canada, Inc.
© 1999 YTV Canada, Inc.
A Corus™ Entertainment Company

Cover art by Miro Sinovcic

Printed in the U.S.A.

For Ashley Grayson,
Dealmaker Extraordinaire

A Letter Home
(Translation)

FROM: Pleskit Meenom, on the emotionally dangerous Planet Earth
TO: Maktel Geebrit, on the relatively sane Planet Hevi-Hevi

Dear Maktel:

Sixth grade is beginning to wear me down. Not only do I have homework and social problems, I have the issue of being the only kid from another planet in my classroom. (Actually, the only kid from another planet *on* the planet, at least, as far as we know. Not to mention the only kid who is bald, purple, and has a *sphen-gnut-ksher* growing out of the top of his head.)

With all that, I was afraid I might not have time to tell you about my latest . . . experience. But it turns out there is an author right here in Syracuse who is interested in writing my stories down for me. He told me he has been making up stories about aliens for years, and that he would love to write about a real one for a change. So Tim and I told him everything that happened as a result of the peanut-butter disaster and let him take it from there.

Believe me, it was a lot easier that way.

I'm sending along a copy of what he wrote.

Since the story is kind of embarrassing, I'm just as glad I didn't have to write it myself.

The biggest surprise was that the Fatherly One was in favor of this book idea. He was so upset with the news stories being written about us that I didn't think he would approve it. But he decided it might be good publicity for our mission. This is something we need, because the mission *is* in trouble. The suspicions you shared with me in your last letter are correct; someone *is* trying to sabotage the Fatherly One's work. Or maybe many some-ones. Anyway, we need to get out all the positive images we can. The Earthlings do not yet realize what hangs in the balance for them, and we are hoping that the books will help them feel more comfortable with us.

Please do not laugh too much when you read about what happened to me. It may seem amusing to you, but it was very painful to live through.

I hope, hope, hope that it works out for you to visit soon. Until then . . . *Fremmix Blee-blom!*

Your pal,
Pleskit

PEANUT BUTTER LOVER BOY

CHAPTER
1

Food Swap

Tim Tompkins stared at his lunch. Peanut butter. Again. He liked peanut butter, but this was getting ridiculous.

"Hey, Pleskit," he said. "What have you got?"

Pleskit Meenom, childling of Meenom Ventrah, ambassador from the planet Hevi-Hevi, looked up. "*Squambul.* Again! I like *squambul*, but this is getting ridiculous."

Tim thought for a moment. He had already had one bad experience with alien food. On the other hand, he *was* interested in all things alien. And he was truly, deeply tired of peanut butter. "Wanna swap?" he asked, holding out his sandwich.

Pleskit looked at the *squambul* pod in his hand.

He looked at Tim's sandwich. A fruity smell drifted out from his *sphen-gnut-ksher*. "Sounds like a good idea to me!"

He glanced over at his bodyguard, Robert Mc-Nally, who was leaning against the wall about ten feet away. The tall black man was looking in their direction. But since, as usual, he was wearing sunglasses, Pleskit couldn't tell if he approved of the swap or not.

Pleskit passed his *squambul* pod to Tim.

Tim passed his sandwich to Pleskit.

The purple boy sniffed at the bread and peanut butter combination. "The aroma is strange, yet enticing," he said after a moment.

"I can't say the same for this," coughed Tim, setting the *squambul* pod on the table.

"You haven't even opened it yet," said Pleskit. "You have to squash it to get the full effect."

"I'm not sure I want the full effect," said Tim, remembering the hilarious photograph of Jordan Lynch's face the first time he had smelled *squambul* that had showed up in *The National News* a week earlier. "Maybe we should swap back."

Pleskit's eyes widened. A smell like burning hair burst from his *sphen-gnut-ksher*. "Please say that you are joking!" he cried, his voice desperate.

"Hey, settle down," said Tim. "It's only lunch. Come on, let's swap back."

Very slowly Pleskit put down the peanut butter sandwich. Placing both hands flat on the table, one on either side of the sandwich, he looked straight into Tim's eyes. "I am asking one more time," he said, his voice deadly serious and tinged with something that sounded like anger. "Are you joking, or do you really mean it?"

Tim blinked. "Uh . . . I guess I was joking." He reached forward and retrieved the *squambul* pod, astonished by his friend's unusual behavior.

Pleskit let out a heavy breath. His face relaxed

into its usual cheerful look. "That's a relief," he said. Then he took a big bite of the sandwich. "Oh, this is good!" he cried excitedly. "Very good!"

Tim looked down at the *squambul* pod and wished he had his sandwich back. *Oh, well*, he told himself. *If I'm going to be an interstellar explorer, I might as well get used to this stuff.* He squashed the pod between his palms. The sharp odor attacked his nose and made his eyes water.

"Lick it fast, while it's still fresh," said Pleskit. "That's when it's best."

Looking at his palm warily, Tim began to lick at the green and purple mess, just as he had seen his friend do on other days. "Hey, this isn't bad!" he said in surprise. "Tastes kind of like chicken."

Later that afternoon, when they were outside for recess, Tim said to Pleskit, "So what was that thing at lunch all about?"

"You mean my distress at your violation of the basic social code?" asked Pleskit.

"I suppose so. I never saw anyone get so bent out of shape about someone wanting to do a trade-back."

"Bent out of shape?" asked Pleskit nervously. He reached up to make sure his *sphen-gnut-ksher* was not somehow disfigured.

"*Upset,*" Tim clarified, ducking as a soccer ball went flying past his head. "You were upset. Why?"

Pleskit replied with a question of his own. "What is the Fatherly One's mission all about, Tim?"

Tim blinked, then said uncertainly, "Uh . . . to establish diplomatic relations, connect Earth to the galaxy, and bring us the benefits of your advanced technology?"

"And why would we want to do that?" persisted Pleskit.

"Because you are a wise and benevolent superior race?"

"So benevolent we have crossed trillions of miles of space just to do you a favor?" Pleskit's face showed amazement. "Do you really think we came all this way simply because we are *nice?*"

"Uh . . . yes?"

"Uh . . . no."

"Then why did you come?"

"I've told you before, this is a trading mission. It is trade that binds the worlds in friendly alliance. The Fatherly One hopes to find something of value on Earth—something that will let you become a trading partner with us."

"You came here to do *business?*" asked Tim in astonishment.

"Of course! Our whole culture is based on trade. And we are taught from the time we leave the egg that a deal is a deal. We do not make a trade and then expect to be able to trade back instantly if we do not like it. Everything would fall apart if we lived like that. That is why I was so shocked when you wanted to go back on our trade in the cafeteria. It was a warning sign of bad cultural habits."

"Okay, I think I'm starting to get it," said Tim. "But what about—"

"Wait!" said Pleskit urgently. *"Look!"*

Tim turned around. Linnsy Vanderhof, his upstairs neighbor, was walking toward them. He shrugged. "What's the big deal? I see Linnsy every day."

"Are you so blind to beauty?" cried Pleskit. "Is your soul so dead to poetry on the hoof?"

Tim turned back. He stared at his friend in concern. "Are you okay, Pleskit?"

"Out of my way!" ordered Pleskit. Pushing past Tim, he puckered his lips and raced toward Linnsy, crying, "Kiss me, baby, *kiss me!*"

CHAPTER
2

Kiss Chase

When Linnsy saw Pleskit coming, she smiled. Then her eyes went wide. Then she shrieked, turned, and ran in the other direction.

"Come back, my little *squiboodlian*, come back!" cried Pleskit.

"Pleskit!" cried McNally. "What are you doing?" Without waiting for an answer, he sprinted after the out-of-control young alien.

"Kiss kiss," cooed Pleskit, racing after Linnsy. "Kiss—"

His words were cut off when McNally caught him from behind and lifted him into the air.

"Let me go!" cried Pleskit, squirming wildly. "I am in pursuit of my beloved!"

"Pleskit!" shouted McNally. "What in heaven's name is wrong with you?"

Pleskit blinked and shook his head. He blinked again, then said, "Why are you holding me, Mc-Nally?"

"Why were you chasing Linnsy?"

"Good question," panted Tim, who had just caught up with them.

"Why was I doing *what?*" asked Pleskit. He sounded genuinely mystified.

"Chasing me!" cried Linnsy. She had stopped about twenty feet from them and was staring at Pleskit with a combination of astonishment and horror. "You said you wanted to kiss me!"

"I *what?*" shouted Pleskit.

"You said you wanted to kiss her," repeated McNally grimly. "You better watch that stuff, buddy. It's not like when I was a kid. Chase a girl on the playground these days, and next thing you know you'll find yourself in court."

"Court?" squeaked Pleskit. His *sphen-gnut-ksher* emitted a smell like rotting carp. "I do not understand." He began to squirm again. "Put me down, please, McNally."

"Can I trust you not to run off?"

"Of course you can."

Eyeing him cautiously, McNally set him down. Pleskit closed his own eyes and took a deep breath. "Could someone please tell me what has been going on?"

"That's what I want to know," said Tim. "We were talking about your weird trade rules when all of a sudden you looked at Linnsy and went all ga-ga. Next thing I knew, you were chasing her."

"Okay, so what was *that* all about, anyway?" asked Linnsy, who had come cautiously back to join them.

Pleskit turned to look at her. His eyes grew wide. "About?" he cried. "It was about *love!*" He darted forward again, crying, "Kiss me, baby, kiss me!"

Linnsy shrieked and ran.

With a quick lunge McNally grabbed Pleskit and lifted him off the ground again. "What the heck is going on here?" he roared.

Pleskit continued to move his feet as if they were still on the ground. "Kiss me, baby, kiss me!" he cried, stretching his arms toward Linnsy.

Other kids had noticed the uproar and were turning in their direction. Most were laughing.

Ms. Weintraub came racing toward them. "What is going on here?" she cried.

"That's just what I want to know," growled McNally.

"Pleskit's lost his mind," said Tim sadly. "He's gone girl crazy. Maybe it's an effect of the atmosphere, or hormones in the water acting on his alien body, or something."

Suddenly Pleskit stopped squirming. "McNally, put me down, please."

"Not again," said McNally firmly. "At least, not without a harness."

"Perhaps you could just put him down and hold his arm, Mr. McNally," said Ms. Weintraub gently.

"Yeah, I suppose I could do that." The muscular bodyguard set Pleskit gently down, but kept a tight grip on his arm. "Don't try anything," he warned.

Pleskit glanced around. "I am confused. Also, I do not feel very well. Perhaps we should go back to the embassy."

"Good idea," said McNally.

"I agree," said Ms. Weintraub. "You're excused for the rest of the day, Pleskit."

Pleskit turned toward Linnsy. "If I have caused you distress, I am most sincerely apologetic."

Jordan Lynch, who had joined the crowd surrounding them said, "You oughtta be, you per—"

"Jordan!" snapped Ms. Weintraub. "Can it!"

Jordan rolled his eyes. So did Brad Kent, his official tagalong and suck-up.

Still holding Pleskit tightly by the arm, McNally led him off the playground.

"Looks like your alien pal has really done it this time, Tompkins," laughed Jordan. "Hey, Linnsy—if you want a lawyer, my dad can put you in touch with someone who specializes in sexual harassment cases."

"Good one, Jordan," said Brad, slapping him on the back.

"Shut up," said Jordan.

Linnsy motioned with her head to Tim. He recognized the sign. Five minutes later, after the group had broken up, he met her at the corner of the school.

"Okay, what was that *really* all about?" she asked.

"I don't have the slightest idea," said Tim. "Honest."

She glared at him suspiciously. "Are you telling me that *wasn't* part of one of your goofy plans?"

"No. Honest. I swear!" said Tim, holding up his hands.

"Well, I didn't like it."

"I don't blame you. But I don't think it was really Pleskit's fault."

"Yeah, that's what guys always say," retorted Linnsy. "Just tell him not to let it happen again."

"I'll pass on the message. Uh . . . you're not going to mention this to your father, are you?"

Tim had always found Linnsy's father a little bit frightening.

Linnsy laughed. "I don't need Dad's help to handle a pair of twerps like you and Pleskit. Just keep in mind that if it happens again, things could get nasty around here fast. Remember, kiss chases can go two ways, buddy."

Tim's eyes widened. "You're not suggesting . . ."

"I'm just saying that vast and widespread social humiliation is a definite possibility if you press me too far."

Tim gulped. "I'll be sure to pass on the message."

CHAPTER
3

Waiting for Whompis

"So what was that all about?" asked McNally when he and Pleskit were in the armored limousine that carried them back and forth from the embassy. "Was this Step One of another wacko scheme you and Tim have cooked up?"

"No!" cried Pleskit earnestly. "I swear by the shards of my egg—and that is an oath that is *meetumlich,* as you can ask the Fatherly One—I am utterly mystified and embarrassed by my own bizarre behavior."

Ralph-the-driver glanced in the rearview mirror but didn't say anything. He never did.

Pleskit put his hand on McNally's arm. "Do you think the Fatherly One will be disturbed?"

"That depends. Do guys on your planet usually have complete personality transplants and start chasing girls around?"

"Never!" cried Pleskit. "That is the girl's job."

"Then he's probably going to be disturbed," said McNally. "At least we don't have any disguised reporters lurking around the school this week; at least, I hope we don't. This is not a story I want to get out." He paused, then added, "Actually, it's the Butt that I'm really worried about."

Pleskit groaned. "The dreaded Ms. Buttsman! I had nearly forgotten that we would have to face her as well."

They were referring to the uptight protocol officer the government had assigned to the embassy.

"She's not going to like this one," said McNally. "I've got a feeling she keeps a copy of *The Politically Correct Handbook* under her pillow. And believe me, Pleskit, this afternoon's display was anything but politically correct."

Pleskit looked at McNally in puzzlement. " 'Politically correct?' Is there going to be a vote about what I did? That is a very alarming thought. Who will do the voting? The class? The PTA? Or maybe—"

"Hold on, Pleskit," said McNally with a laugh. "Politically correct is just a way of referring to things you're not supposed to say or do for fear you might offend someone somewhere somehow.

It's a good idea that went bad when it got out of control."

"I know how *that* feels," said Pleskit ruefully.

The limo turned into Thorncraft Park. At the top of the park's central hill was the embassy. Dangling from a tall, silvery hook, it looked something like a flying saucer attached to the top part of a coat hanger. At the base of the hill was a tunnel that allowed the limo to bypass the crowds that still gathered every day to gaze in wonder at the home of the first aliens to make open contact with Earth.

When Pleskit and McNally stepped out of the elevator that had carried them from the limousine's underground parking space to the embassy foyer, they found Ms. Buttsman waiting for them. Her face was grim, her arms were crossed, and she was tapping her right foot.

"I've been expecting you," she said coldly. "Principal Grand called a few minutes ago to fill me in on today's events. I'm sure your Fatherly One will have a great deal to say to you about this matter later on, Pleskit."

"How much later?" asked Pleskit nervously.

"That depends. Right now we are gathering to greet the ambassador's new assistant. He is due to arrive any moment."

"Beezle Whompis is actually coming?" asked

Pleskit excitedly. "I had begun to think he would never get here!"

"We received word just a little while ago. Really, I don't think your communication systems are quite as spectacular as you would like us to believe. Anyway, your Fatherly One was fussing about getting you home from school to be part of the welcoming, so it's good that you are here. I haven't yet told him the disgraceful reason *why* you happened to come home right now. Time enough for that later." She drew in a deep breath and shook her head. "Really, Pleskit, I *am* surprised at you—though I guess I shouldn't be."

"That's all right, Ms. Buttsman," said McNally. "I'm continually surprised at you as well, even though I really ought to be over it by this time."

Ms. Buttsman shot him a cold look. "Walk this way," she said.

Pleskit could hardly keep from laughing out loud when McNally followed the woman, doing a perfect imitation of her walk.

The embassy staff had gathered around the shift-stone table in the main meeting room. Shhh-foop, the queen of the kitchen, was singing to herself and waving her orange tentacles in time to her song. Barvgis, round as a beach ball and slimy as an earthworm, sat at the end of the table, munching a gnawstick, which he did whenever he had to go too long without actually eating. The Fatherly One, standing in his usual place, nodded when he saw Pleskit and McNally come in. Even the brain of the Grandfatherly One had been put in its Transport Device and brought into the room.

"When will Beezle Whompis's ship arrive?" asked Pleskit, once he had taken his place beside his Fatherly One.

"He's not coming by ship," said Meenom.

"Then how is he getting here?" asked Pleskit, confused.

"Electronic transfer," said Barvgis, pointing to an ornate metallic device suspended from the ceiling. Dozens of curving purple and blue pipes wound and twisted and looped around one another, finally merging into three separate devices that looked like strangely flaring crowns with insets of red glass.

The bases of the "crowns" were pointing to the center of the table.

Suddenly the device began to glow.

"Quiet!" ordered Meenom. "It's starting!"

CHAPTER
4

Alien Arrival

A low hum filled the room. The glow of the pipes grew more intense. The "crowns" pulsed with light.

The hum changed to a crackling sound. The air seemed charged with power.

"Oh, my my my my my," sang Shhh-foop, pressing three tentacles to her face.

ZZZZZAAAAAAP!

Streams of light flowed from the crowns, merging in the center of the table. A hazy cloud began to develop. Filled with dancing points of light, it swirled around itself, the points of light moving faster and faster.

A form began to take shape, tall and lean.

A hissing, sizzling sound from the transfer device was followed by a final burst of energy.

The device went silent and dark.

"E.T., phone home," whispered McNally in awe.

The haze continued to swirl, the form in the center of it slowly becoming more clear and specific until with a sudden sucking sound the mist and the light collapsed inward.

Beezle Whompis had arrived.

The aliens burst into applause—each showing approval in the way specific to his, her, or its planet. Meenom belched heartily. Barvgis slapped his hands loudly against his own shoulders, shouting *"Pooong! Pooong! Poong!"* Shhh-foop swirled her tentacles, causing them to emit a hissing sound. Pleskit burped, too. But at the same time he felt a small twist of fear, which caused him to feel angry with himself. He had already lived on three previous worlds (four, if you counted Geembol Seven, which he preferred not to). He knew enough not to fear someone merely because of appearance.

Even so, keeping fear at bay was not always easy.

He studied the newcomer, knowing that, for beings of goodwill, knowledge usually displaces fear.

Beezle Whompis was at least seven feet tall and completely bald. His enormous, deepset eyes were the most prominent feature of his thin, almost cadaverous, face. His skin, which looked like dry, yellowed parchment, was stretched tightly over his sunken cheeks. Three rounded nostrils in the otherwise flat center of his face gave only the tiniest hint of a nose. An elegant robe hung from his bony shoulders, reaching nearly to his feet.

He gazed at the beings gathered around the table, then shook himself from head to foot, as if he had just experienced a chill.

"Well, *that* was an interesting trip," he said, seeming to speak mostly to himself. Turning to Meenom, he bowed slightly and added, "Beezle Whompis, reporting for service."

"Welcome, Beezle Whompis," said Meenom. "We have been eagerly awaiting your arrival."

"I am pleased to be here," said Beezle Whompis, inclining his head slightly. "My apologies for the delay. Things at my last job became unexpectedly complicated. Just one problem after another, if you know what I mean." He waved his skeletal fingers in front of his face in a complicated gesture.

"Well, if that's what you're used to, you're going to feel right at home here," muttered McNally.

Ms. Buttsman shot him an icy glare.

"I have never seen one of those transfers done before," said Barvgis. "It was very impressive."

Beezle Whompis bowed his head in acknowledgment of the compliment. Then he shimmered and disappeared. A moment later he was standing on the floor next to Ms. Buttsman. She uttered a tiny shriek, then clapped her hand to her mouth and began to blush.

"Forgive me, Ms. Buttsman," said Meenom. "I should have given you more information regarding our new staff member. Beezle Whompis is a . . ." He paused, as if searching for a word.

"Allow me," said Beezle Whompis. Turning to Ms. Buttsman, he said, "I am a—"

The last "word" of his sentence was a harsh, grinding sound, like static on a radio. He smiled, or made something like a smile, since though his mouth curved up, it still drooped at the corners. "Think of me as a discorporate entity. My people do not have bodies, at least, not as you use the term. I take on this form merely as a matter of . . . politeness. I have found it is easier for the flesh-bound to relate to me if they can see me like this."

"How . . . interesting," said Ms. Buttsman, edging away from him.

"I would shake your hand in standard Earth greeting," continued Beezle Whompis, "but doing so would cause all your hair to stand on end, which my studies have indicated you would not appreciate."

"Sounds like fun to me," said McNally as Ms. Buttsman patted her hair nervously.

"I am most eager to experience all of you," said Beezle Whompis, turning to face the others at the table. "But first, Ambassador, I beg a moment in private. I must deliver an urgent message."

CHAPTER
5

Linnsy's Mom

Tim and Linnsy walked home from school together that afternoon, something that had not happened much during the last two years, despite the fact that they lived in the same apartment building. They had started to pick up the habit again since Pleskit's arrival—mostly because there was so often something disturbing or confusing they needed to discuss.

"Okay," said Linnsy. "If Pleskit chasing me on the playground today wasn't part of one of your wacky schemes, then what *was* it all about?"

"I don't have the slightest idea," said Tim.

Linnsy frowned. "You do realize this means big trouble?"

Tim looked blank. "Just because he chased you around once?"

"Twice, actually. But the reason it means trouble is not because he chased me, but because he doesn't seem to have any idea why he did it—which means he might do it again!"

"I'd been thinking about that possibility," said Tim glumly. "I was hoping I was wrong."

"Well, you were right for a change. The question now is, what can we do about it?"

But for that, Tim had no answer.

They stopped on the bridge to stare at the embassy dangling above the hill in Thorncraft Park.

"What do you suppose it's like to live in there?" asked Linnsy, still awed by the sight.

"Only the coolest thing in the universe," said Tim, who loved visiting the embassy with all its weird, otherworldly furnishings.

"I bet it's lonely," said Linnsy. "I bet Pleskit thinks about home a lot."

"That's so girl," said Tim.

"And you're so dork," replied Linnsy. She gave him a little punchie-wunchie, which was what she called it when she socked him on the biceps to try to get him to straighten up. "Come on, let's go see if my mother baked today."

"Why should this day be different from any

other day?" asked Tim, torn between annoyance at the punchie-wunchie and delight at being asked up to Linnsy's place. He could not remember a time he had gone up after school when Mrs. Vanderhof *didn't* have something just coming out of the oven. Only he hadn't gone up there very often in the last year or so, after he and Linnsy had drifted into different social groups. (Well, Linnsy had drifted into a social group; Tim had just drifted, until Pleskit arrived and he found someone as weird as himself to hang out with.)

"How nice to see you, Mr. Timothy," said Mrs. Vanderhof when he and Linnsy came through the door. ("Mr. Timothy" had been her nickname for Tim from before he was even in kindergarten.) "You're just in time for some butterscotch brownies."

"Ah," said Tim, sitting down at the kitchen table. "Just what I was hoping for!" He picked up one of the brownies and took an enormous bite. It was as rich and delicious as he remembered.

"So, how was your day?" asked Mrs. Vanderhof, pulling out a chair to join them.

Linnsy glanced at Tim uncertainly. He paused, chewed thoughtfully, then gave a nod that indicated he thought she should spill the whole story.

"Well," she said slowly, "it was sort of weird."

Then she told what had happened with Pleskit on the playground.

"Goodness," cried Mrs. Vanderhof, putting her hand to her chest. "It sounds like the last time *I* went crazy."

Tim choked on his brownie.

CHAPTER
6

The Fatherly One

Pleskit watched in dismay as the Fatherly One and Beezle Whompis left the meeting room to head for the Fatherly One's private office.

"What do you suppose the message is?" he asked, once the door had closed behind them.

Ms. Buttsman—who seemed to be recovering from her shock at meeting Beezle Whompis—said primly, "I'm sure it's adult business and no concern of yours, Pleskit."

"You are a source of unending joy, Ms. Buttsman," said McNally.

Ms. Buttsman gave him a tight smile. "Don't forget that when Meenom is done with Beezle Whompis he will want to speak to Pleskit about what happened at school today. I expect he will want to discuss it with you, too, Mr. McNally." She looked around the room. "Well! That's settled, I think. Mr. Whompis has made it here safely, so why don't we all just get back to our jobs?"

And with that she left the room.

"Someone must be feeding that lady bad food," sang Shhh-foop, whirling several of her tentacles. She turned to Pleskit. "Singing of food— would you like a snackie-doodle, my little Pleskit-pie?"

"Sounds like a good idea," said Pleskit glumly.

"I don't suppose you have anything for me?" asked Barvgis hopefully.

"Of course," sang Shhh-foop. "Always lots to eat for the pleasingly plump. And perhaps a cup of coffee for the handsome guarder of Pleskit's body?"

"Uh, sure," said McNally nervously. He liked Shhh-foop. But her attempts at coffee had all been hideous failures.

The little group had no sooner gathered in the kitchen than a red light flashed above the door. They heard a slight hissing sound. Then a sharp smell drifted through the room.

Barvgis sighed. "I guess my snack will have to wait, Shhh-foop. I have been summoned."

"Come back soon!" sang Shhh-foop, waving

her tentacles in farewell. Then she slapped two of them against the counter to summon the coffeepot.

Barvgis left the room, mournfully patting his very round midsection as he went. Shhh-foop slid across the floor with a cup of coffee. She placed it delicately in front of McNally, then slid back a few feet and watched him anxiously, several of her tentacles twitching just a bit.

McNally sniffed it, then raised it to his lips and took a cautious sip. His eyes widened, and he looked slightly terrified. "Not quite, Shhh-foop," he said hoarsely. Staring at the steaming coffee as if it might bite him, he returned the cup to the table.

"Woe, woe is she who cannot coax true joy from the bean of caffeine for Just McNally," crooned Shhh-foop sadly as she slid back to the counter. She returned a moment later with a tray of squeaking purple cubes, which she placed in front of Pleskit. *Pak-skwardles,* she sang proudly.

"Great!" cried Pleskit, scooping one into his mouth. He turned to his bodyguard. "Want some, McNally? They're delicious."

"Uh—I think I'll go to my room now," said McNally. "I'll catch you later, Pleskit. Good luck with your Fatherly One."

Pleskit's face grew suddenly serious. "Oy," he

said, using a word he had learned from the brain of his Grandfatherly One.

It did not take long for the summons to come. When it did, Pleskit popped a last *pak-skwardle* into his mouth for comfort, then trudged out of the kitchen. His pet Veeblax, a strange little shapeshifter, joined him in the corridor. It walked beside him, cooing sympathetically.

To reach Meenom's office Pleskit first had to pass through an outer office, where Meenom's assistant held guard. When Pleskit reached this outer office, he was startled to see Beezle Whompis already sitting in the chair that had been occupied by Mikta-makta-mookta, until her villainous plans to sabotage the mission had been revealed.

The new assistant nodded as Pleskit came in. "Your Fatherly One said to send you in the moment you got here," he said. Then he vanished—only to pop up directly next to Pleskit, which caused the purple boy to jump in surprise.

"Sorry," said Beezle Whompis. "I should remember it takes you physical beings a while to get used to that. Listen, I've gone over the messages from school today, and the situation is not pleasant. I thought I should warn you that your parental unit is most distressed."

He vanished again, only to reappear in the chair where he had been sitting a moment earlier.

Pleskit blinked and headed into the office, the Veeblax at his heels.

Meenom's command pod was floating halfway between floor and ceiling.

"You wished to see me, Fatherly One?" asked Pleskit, looking up and feeling small.

"I have had a disturbing report from the school, my childling." He paused, then added significantly. "Another one."

Pleskit hung his head. "I have no excuse, parent/mentor. An unbearable urge came over me most unexpectedly. At first I did not even realize what was happening."

Meenom burped a command, and the pod drifted gently to the floor. He stepped out and put his hands on Pleskit's shoulders. "These are difficult times for the mission," he said. His voice was somber, serious. "I need you to exercise caution and control right now, Pleskit. Especially control. Obviously it will take time for us to learn all the little ways in which things in this planet's environment may affect us. But you cannot use that as an excuse! You must control yourself. These are perilous times for us."

The fear Pleskit felt now had nothing to do with the Fatherly One's anger. "I do not understand," he said quietly.

"I will explain," said Meenom.

CHAPTER
7

Crazy Talk

Linnsy looked at her mother angrily. "Mom!" she said, between clenched teeth.

"Oh, for heaven's sake, Linnsy," said Mrs. Vanderhof. "There is no reason for Mr. Timothy not to know about what happened."

"Yes, there is," said Linnsy.

Ms. Vanderhof shook her head slightly. "I refuse to take part in my own repression," she said. Her voice was calm, but very serious. "If more people were open about this kind of thing, there wouldn't be so much shame and fear attached to it—which would mean that more people would get help when they needed it."

Linnsy sighed, rolled her eyes, and crossed

her arms over her chest. "I suppose you're going to talk about this whether I want you to or not."

"It makes a good test, dear," said Mrs. Vanderhof cheerfully. "You'll find that people who can't handle it aren't worth hanging around with." She turned to Tim. "Do you remember a night about two years ago that your mom got a sudden call to come up here?"

"Not really," said Tim. Then he blinked and said, "Wait, was that the time you went away for a couple of weeks? Whoa! Don't tell me you were in the loony bin all that time!"

"See what I mean?" cried Linnsy.

Tim's eyes widened in horror as he realized what he had just blurted out. "Ack! I'm sorry! I didn't mean to say that! It just . . . I mean . . . Omigosh, I am *so* sorry."

He glanced down at the floor, vaguely hoping a giant hole would open and swallow him into another dimension.

Mrs. Vanderhof sighed and shook her head wearily. "I'd be angrier, if I wasn't so used to it, Mr. Timothy."

"So why can't you just keep quiet about it?" asked Linnsy savagely.

"No, I can handle it," said Tim. "Really I can. I was just startled. Honest."

"Besides, when you get right down to it, I really was loony at the time," said Mrs. Vanderhof. "Someone listening to me might have found my ramblings pretty hilarious, or pretty scary. Or both, I suppose. For me, it was exciting and scary all at once. I felt I knew things that no one else knew, understood the world in a way that no one else ever had."

"She left messages all over the house, explaining the secret meaning of things," said Linnsy.

"If I remember correctly, the toaster held the secret to world peace," said Mrs. Vanderhof with a laugh. "Yet for all that I felt I had secret knowledge, at the same time I was terrified. I knew I was out of control, but didn't know what to do about it." She turned and looked out the window for a moment. "I imagine it was pretty scary for those around me as well."

"You're not kidding," said Linnsy. She turned to Tim. "When I got home from school that day, Mom was sitting in the middle of the floor. She had her suitcase next to her, her camera around her neck, and a flashlight in her hands. When I asked what was going on, she said she was waiting for the aliens to come and take her back where she came from."

"But that was two years before the aliens had even made contact," said Tim. Then he blinked. "Oh," he said softly. "I see."

Mrs. Vanderhof smiled ruefully. "I had found a card inviting Linnsy to a birthday party with an alien theme. In my condition, I took it to mean some aliens were inviting me to be their queen."

"When I walked in, she was singing the theme song from 'Tarbox Moon Warriors,' " Linnsy said. "She told me she had made a week's worth of cookies, but after that I would be on my own because she had to return to her true home in the stars."

"Actually, dear, I think I told you that you could come along."

Linnsy laughed. "Yeah, but only if I ate a dozen of your secret rocket cookies first." She turned to Tim. "I was so terrified. Dad was out of town on a business trip. And Mom seemed so convinced of what she was saying that I almost believed her—though I got over that when she started having a conversation with my teddy bear."

"I thought he was Captain Norf-Norf," explained Mrs. Vanderhof. "I think that was when Linnsy called your mom and asked for help."

"But you seem so—" Tim searched for a word. "So *normal*," he finally said, somewhat lamely.

"I am normal! At least, I am when my blood chemistry is working properly. I have a condition called manic-depression, and I take a drug called lithium to keep it under control. It's a true miracle. When my chemistry is off, I can leave reality so far behind it looks as if I'll never see it again. But as soon as they get my dose properly adjusted, I start coming back in for a landing."

"So, are all crazy people like that?" Tim closed his eyes in embarrassment. "Sorry. But you know what I mean."

Mrs. Vanderhof shook her head. "*Crazy* comes in a lot of different flavors. Some of the people in what you called 'the loony bin' are in for the long haul—or at least, they are until some breakthrough in treatment occurs. Others are folk who have had their cup of sorrow filled way beyond the brim; they've made a temporary retreat from sanity because it's more than they can cope with. And some are like me, people with a short-term problem that can be fixed fairly simply by getting their chemistry straightened out. The thing is, despite all we've learned, most of the world still reacts to mental problems as if there is some deep shame about them. But what I deal with is no more shameful than diabetes or a heart problem."

"In your opinion," said Linnsy.

"In reality," her mother replied firmly. "The problem is, people haven't had time to get used to that idea. A hundred years ago odds are good I would have spent my life in an institution—just for lack of the right medicine!"

A new question, a somewhat frightening one, occurred to Tim. Trying not to sound too nervous, he asked, "This condition, isn't, uh . . . catching, is it?"

Mrs. Vanderhof laughed. "You can't catch it just by being near me, Tim. Can't catch it at all, actually. It's something you're born with, though it sometimes takes a long time to show up."

"Okay, I've got the picture. But what does this all have to do with Pleskit?"

Mrs. Vanderhof shrugged and reached for a brownie. "I'm not sure. It's just that, from your description, he moved in and out of this strange condition so fast that it sounded like a speeded-up version of what I sometimes go through." She glanced at him and laughed. "Oh, stop looking so worried, Tim. I went seven years between my first 'episode' and the one I told you about. I'm not going to wack-out on you in the next thirty seconds. The good news is, we're understanding more about the problem all the time. I know your dream is to explore the vast reaches of outer space. But the truth is, there's a whole universe inside our heads that we've barely begun to discover." She tapped him on the forehead. "Between your ears lies a vast, uncharted wilderness."

"That's definitely true for Tim," Linnsy said with a laugh. "Who knows what weirdness lurks between *those* ears?"

Tim's search for a withering response was interrupted by the phone.

"It's for you, Mr. Timothy," Mrs. Vanderhof said a moment later.

Tim took the receiver.

It was his mother. "Tim, I think you'd better get down here," she said. "Pronto!"

CHAPTER
8

Communication

When Tim entered his apartment, he found a large purple package sitting in the center of the living room floor.

"It's from the embassy," said his mother. "Ralph-the-driver dropped it off about five minutes ago. He said Pleskit wanted you to open it as soon as possible. I figured you'd want to know right away. He also left a note," she added, passing Tim a small purple envelope.

"This is too cool!" cried Tim, his eyes sparkling. "I wonder what it is?" After stuffing the envelope into his pocket, he grabbed the package and began trying to open it.

Five minutes later, snarling with frustration, he

was still trying. The wrapping material, whatever it was, had proved impossible to cut or tear in any way.

"May I offer a suggestion?" asked his mother gently.

"What?" snapped Tim.

"Oh, never mind. If you can't speak civilly, I'll keep my stupid adult thoughts to myself."

Tim sighed. "Sorry. What's your suggestion?"

"Why not check what's in the envelope?"

Feeling foolish, Tim pulled the envelope from his pocket. Unlike the package, it opened easily.

Tim:

Greetings and good wishes!

I have finally arranged for us to have a more effective method of communication than your primitive telephone system provides. At last I will be able to see you and smell you when we talk, rather than simply hearing you! (You will be able to smell me as well. However, I know this is not a particularly effective means of communication for Earthlings, so you can switch off the odor-emitter if it bothers you.)

Batteries are not included, mostly because they are embargoed technology. I'm not sure why I can send you the communicator and not the batteries, unless the Trading Federation has determined that your scientists might be able to figure out how to make the batteries, while the communicator would be beyond them. Anyway, we had to come up with another power source, which is part of why this has taken so long. Barvgis finally reconfigured the device so you can plug it into a standard Earth socket. It disturbed him to do so, but he said it was the best solution, inelegant though it appears.

To open the package just run your fingertip along the edges of the box. It has been cued to your personal chemistry, which we have on record from your trips to the embassy.

Please contact me as soon as you have the unit up and running. I had a very disturbing conversation with the Fatherly One this afternoon, and I want to discuss it with you.

Looking forward to seeing/hearing/smelling you.

Fremmix Bleeblom!

Your pal,
Pleskit

Tim looked at his fingertip, not certain he liked the idea that the aliens had so much information on file about him. Too curious to spend much time worrying about that, he ran his fingertip along the edges of the box, then gasped as the sides, top, and bottom rolled into small tubes. Without a sound the tubes slid one into another. A second later all that remained of the box was something that looked like a long, purple straw.

"I wonder how this thing works," said Mrs. Tompkins, picking up the slender tube. "I'd love to have a bunch of these come Christmas time. I'd save hours of wrapping!"

Tim was too intrigued by the contents of the box to answer. The base of the object was circular, about an inch thick and maybe eight or nine inches across. Mounted on this base was something that would have looked like the monitor for a computer, if monitors were round and no thicker than a penny. On the base was a single rounded button, purple. From the back side of the machine extended a plain brown cord.

"Gotta go check this out," said Tim. Picking up the machine, he carried it into his room. It took him a few minutes to clear a spot among the welter of comic books, action figures, and dirty laundry where he could set the machine.

He plugged it in.

Nothing happened.

He reached out and touched the button on the base.

The circular screen began to glow. A pair of small boxes folded out from the base, then two metallic tentacles stretched up from the boxes. They reminded Tim of the extensions that came from the brainvat of Pleskit's Grandfatherly One.

"Do you wish to make contact?" asked a pleasant voice.

"Yes!" shouted Tim, so excited he couldn't stay in his chair.

"Such volume is not necessary," said the voice, sounding as if it were wincing. "With whom do you wish to be connected?"

"Pleskit."

"Noted and logged. I will let you know when contact is—" The voice was cut off. Pleskit's face appeared on the screen. "Tim!" he said happily. "You got it working!"

"This is so cool!" said Tim. "Can you see me?"

Pleskit blinked, as if surprised by the question. "Of course. That was the point. I can smell you, too, which makes the communication much more complete—though the odor from your underwear pile sends more information than I really want to know." He leaned closer to the screen. "Are you alone?"

"Yeah, I'm in my room. Mom tries not to come in here, on account of it makes her so upset."

"Good. I need to talk to you."

"What's up? Wait! Did you get in much trouble about what happened at school today?"

"The Fatherly One was surprisingly understanding—though he did get cranky about the fact that I brought the Veeblax into his office with me. But listen, Tim. There are other things going on here—things that are very disturbing."

Tim frowned. "That doesn't sound so good."

"It's not. The Fatherly One's new assistant arrived today—"

"Beezle Whompis is here?" interrupted Tim. "I was beginning to think he was never coming. Is he cool?"

"Please, do not start again with 'cool,'" said Pleskit, who still had not been able to totally grasp the idea. "Let's just say he is . . . unusual. The important thing right now is that he brought a message from the Interplanetary Trading Federation." Pleskit took a deep breath. "Things do not look good for the mission."

Tim felt a cold chill. "Why not?"

"The beings who are monitoring us feel that the Fatherly One is not progressing rapidly enough toward his goals."

"Geez, Pleskit, you've only been here a few weeks. What do they want?"

Pleskit looked uncomfortable. "It's not so much what he hasn't done as it is how many things have gone wrong. There have been a remarkable number of . . . incidents, given the brief time we have been here."

"Hey, it's not like Mikta-makta-mookta was your fault," said Tim indignantly. "She was *assigned* to you guys by the Trading Federation."

"That is true," Pleskit agreed. "However, even in an advanced civilization, people like to shift blame whenever they can. And the Fatherly One makes an easy target because of what happened on Geembol Seven."

"Which I still want to know more about," said Tim quickly.

The communication device emitted a sudden gust of odor. Tim flinched back. "Man, Pleskit," he said, waving his hand in front of his face. "If you don't want to talk about it, just say so. You don't have to stink up my whole room!"

"Sorry. Involuntary reaction. Tap the top of the device twice if you want to turn off the odor transmitter."

"Whew," said Tim a minute later, still waving his hand in front of his face. "That's better. So, what do the top guys at the Trading Federation want?"

"Well, Beezle Whompis says the best thing we could do is show real progress in finding something that can be used for interstellar trade. If things don't get better soon, the Fatherly One may lose his franchise."

"Just how bad would that be?"

"Very bad for us—even worse for you."

"What does *that* mean?"

"Most beings who have studied the situation— and there's not that many of them, because Earth is still considered a very minor planet—think it would be better just to colonize the planet."

"Colonize it?" asked Tim uneasily.

"Take it over," said Pleskit bluntly. "The Fatherly One is considered a real *beezledorf* for the way he wants to deal with you. But he staked the first claim, so his wishes have to be honored—unless the Federation decides he has not exploited the franchise properly."

"And if they decide that?"

"Then we're out, and someone else—someone much tougher—takes over the planet."

"Yikes!"

"Precisely. The problem is finding something worth trading. Frankly, Earth does not have much to offer. Certainly not your technology, which is far behind ours. You might provide a good work force, but that would take lots of training."

"What about our natural resources?" asked Tim. "Haven't you guys all like plundered your planets and ruined your ecologies and stuff?"

Pleskit laughed. "What do you think we are, idiots? Earth *is* potentially one of the fairest and richest planets in the galaxy. Unfortunately, it is currently also one of the worst managed. According to the Fatherly One, the first survey team wept in frustration when they saw what you people have done to the place."

"Well, that makes me feel just wonderful," said Tim.

"Don't take it personally," replied Pleskit. "However, it would probably be just as well if your room was never exposed to off-planet scrutiny."

"Ha very ha."

Pleskit smiled. "Oh, good. I made a joke! But do not worry, the problem at the moment has much less to do with you than it does with me. Today's events at school only added to the sense that the mission is being mismanaged. Botched." His face got very serious. "Tim, I do not want to be responsible for costing the Fatherly One yet another planetary assignment!"

"I don't think what happened today was really your fault," said Tim, remembering his conversation with Mrs. Vanderhof.

"Well, I certainly didn't do it on purpose."

"Right, so the question is—" Tim stopped. His eyes widened. "Hold on! I think I've got it!"

CHAPTER
9

Experiment

"You think you've got what?" asked Pleskit in alarm. "Do you mean it's catching? Are you going to start chasing girls around, too?"

Tim snorted. "As if! I mean, I think I know what set you off today."

"What?"

"Think about it. What did you do today that was different than most days? Think lunch, Pleskit."

"*Peanut butter!*" cried Pleskit. "I ate your peanut-butter sandwich." His *sphen-gnut-ksher* bent sideways in a questioning gesture. "Do you really think that was the source of my bizarre actions?"

"Makes as much sense as anything else. Do you have any way to check it out?"

"Certainly. We can explore the idea the same way we would explore any other hypothesis—by conducting an experiment."

Tim wrinkled his brow. "What do you have in mind?"

"It should be obvious. We put me in a room with a female of your species, feed me peanut butter, and see what happens."

"Not unless we tie you down first!" cried Tim in alarm.

"An excellent idea!" said Pleskit, emitting the slightly spicy odor of agreement. (The smell did not reach Tim, of course, since he had turned off the odor receiver.) "Can you arrange for Linnsy to come down to your apartment? I will see if I can get McNally to bring me over."

"Good. Then you can give me some more instructions for using this communication thingie," said Tim. "I'm going by the seat of my pants right now."

"There is no need to show it your backside!" cried Pleskit. "I did not think you Earthlings had sufficient control of your farting mechanism to give the device commands that way, so Barvgis reprogrammed it to be more sensitive to spoken language. I am sorry I underestimated your communication skills."

Tim sighed. "I just meant . . . oh, never mind.

I'll call you back as soon as I've talked to Linnsy. If you don't hear from me in ten minutes, you better call me, because it may mean I'm having trouble with the machine. Hmm. Better make it fifteen. Convincing Linnsy may take a while."

"I may have the same problem with McNally," said Pleskit. "He is officially off-duty. Therefore, some pleading is likely to be required to get him to bring me over." He made a long, multitoned belch, smiled, and said, "That means: Talk to you/see you/smell you soon."

The machine went dark.

Tim went to call Linnsy on the regular phone.

Linnsy's first response was pretty much what Tim had expected.

"You want me to *what?*"

"We want you to participate in an experiment that could help determine the future of earth-alien relationships," said Tim, trying to sound reassuring. "Controlled conditions. Perfectly safe. Could be crucial to life as we know it."

"Hold on," said Linnsy. "Let me check the weather report. Aha! Just as I thought. 'Cloudy, with a chance of wackos.' "

"Linnsy!"

"Tim!"

Click.

He called her back.

"Hi. It's me."

"Like, big surprise."

"Come on, Linns. There's nothing to worry about. McNally will be here, and Pleskit will be . . . immobilized. We just need to check out my theory."

"You need to check out your brain!"

Click.

He called her back. Before he could even say her name, she shouted, "Will you stop bothering me?"

"Not until you help us save the world."

"Give me one good reason," said Linnsy, who had actually decided she would help two phone calls ago.

"Saving the world isn't enough of a reason?" yelped Tim.

"Give me one good reason this idiotic idea has anything to do with saving the world."

Tim hesitated, then said, "Because Pleskit's Fatherly One is the good guy. If he gets recalled by the Interplanetary Trading Federation, the next Trader who gets the Earth franchise may decide we should be a colony instead of a partner."

Linnsy went silent for so long that Tim began to

wonder if she had put the phone down and walked away. Finally she said, "Tim, are you messing with me on this? Because if you are—"

"Tarbox Honor, Linnsy," said Tim, which effectively cut off her question. Tim might like to wiggle around on the edges of reality, but Linnsy knew that he was deadly serious about the Tarbox oath.

She sighed. "I'll be there."

It was early evening. Gathered in the living room of the Tompkins apartment were Tim, Pleskit, McNally, and Tim's mother.

Linnsy was waiting in the kitchen.

"Are you sure this is a good idea?" said Mrs. Tompkins nervously.

"Mom, I've told you what's at stake. Besides, McNally is here to keep Pleskit in line—which he won't even need to do unless my theory is correct."

"I concur with Tim's analysis," said Pleskit. He was sitting in a straight-backed wooden chair. McNally stood behind him, hands resting on the back of the chair, just above Pleskit's shoulders, ready to grab him if necessary.

Mrs. Tompkins sighed. "What about you, Mr. McNally?"

The bodyguard shrugged. "I think it's worth a shot."

Mrs. Tompkins stepped forward and gingerly placed a peanut-butter sandwich on the tray-table that Tim had set up by Pleskit's chair.

"Divine aroma," said Pleskit, picking up the sandwich and sniffing at it.

He took a bite.

Everyone watched him anxiously.

"I think I should probably eat the whole sandwich," he said. "Also, even if this is the source of the problem, it may take a while for it to kick in."

He took another bite of the sandwich, and then another.

Tim, too impatient to wait for him to finish, motioned for Linnsy to come into the room.

The moment she entered, Pleskit put down the sandwich. He sat back in his chair as if he had been stunned. "Oh, you beautiful baby!" he muttered. Then, leaping from his chair, he cried, "Come to poppa, my little *bliddki!*"

McNally grabbed Pleskit's shoulders and forced him back into the chair.

"Let me go!" cried Pleskit, squirming beneath his bodyguard's grip. "Love calls. Biology beckons. Frisko the god of love has pierced my *clinkus* with his flaming arrows. I have seen my future, and she is Linnsy!"

"Pleskit!" snapped McNally. "Get ahold of yourself."

"You'd better go back in the kitchen, Linnsy," said Tim quietly.

Eyes wide, Linnsy slipped out of the room. As soon as she was gone, Pleskit slumped back in his chair.

"Hypothesis proved," said Tim. "Pleskit can *not* handle his peanut butter."

"That's the worst allergic reaction I've seen since Aunt Louise accidentally ate the shrimp salad," said Mrs. Tompkins, her voice a little shaky. "I think I need some coffee. Would you like a cup, Mr. McNally?"

"Love some. But I'd better wait till we're sure Pleskit's under control. I don't dare let go of him yet."

Pleskit groaned. "This is the most humiliating thing I have ever experienced. Please carry my apologies to Linnsy."

"It's okay!" shouted Linnsy from the kitchen. "Just don't get near me for the time being."

"I am a walking social catastrophe," said Pleskit mournfully.

"Nah, you're just another victim of biology," said McNally. "If we keep you away from peanut butter, you should be fine."

That, however, proved to be more easily said than done.

CHAPTER
10

Things Get Stickier

"Pleskit Meenom, please report to the office. I repeat: Pleskit Meenom, please report to the office."

"Zgribnick!" muttered Pleskit. His *sphen-gnut-ksher* emitted a smell that reminded Tim of a piece of baloney he had once accidentally left under his bed for several months.

McNally stood to go with him.

"Looks like your reputation has caught up with you, lover boy," hooted Jordan. "Remember, we don't go for sexual harassment in this school—especially not from aliens."

"Pack it in, Jordan!" snapped Ms. Weintraub. "Pleskit has already explained what happened yesterday."

*   *   *

Mr. Grand sat behind his desk, looking very serious.

Pleskit stood in front of him, feeling very nervous.

McNally leaned against the back wall, showing no expression at all.

"I have heard disturbing rumors about an event that occurred on the playground yesterday," said Mr. Grand, steepling his fingertips in front of his face.

"I can explain everything, sir," said Pleskit.

"Please do."

Pleskit did. When he was done, Mr. Grand shook his head and said sadly, "Really, Pleskit, I expected better of you."

"But it's true!" cried Pleskit.

"Your behavior was bad enough," Mr. Grand said, taking a sourball out of the jar he always kept on his desk. "But trying to shift the blame in this silly fashion—*peanut butter*, for heaven's sake!—is even worse. Better by far, my young interstellar traveler, to simply accept responsibility for your actions. That is more honorable, more manly. It is the Earthling way."

He bit down on the sourball. "Now, I want a promise from you that this behavior will not be repeated. I will work very hard to keep word of it from leaking to the press—you know what kind of trouble we have when they get their noses onto something like this. But you have to work with me here, Pleskit. You simply can't go around exhibiting such outrageous behavior and expect to have no consequences."

"Am I going to be punished?" asked Pleskit uneasily.

"Not this time. But if it should happen again—well, punishment aside, I fear we could end up in court! The world does not take such behavior lightly these days. Now, no more of this nonsense about peanut butter. Simply control yourself, and everything will be fine. If you feel an urge to chase one of the girls, take a deep breath, count to ten, and just say no. That's what I always used to do. You can go now."

That afternoon the girls on the playground giggled and pointed when Pleskit walked by. Seeing this, Linnsy made it a point to go hang out with Pleskit, which seemed to calm things down a bit. After a few minutes Misty Longacres and Rafaella Cruz wandered over to talk with him as well.

The next day Ms. Weintraub announced that the science fair would take place earlier than usual this year.

"You'll need to start thinking about your projects soon," she said. "Here's a list of possibilities."

"Pleskit can do something on peanut-butter allergies," said Jordan with a snicker.

"Allergies are serious business," said Larrabe Hicks solemnly.

"So is terminal dorkhood," said Jordan.

"What, exactly, is a science fair?" asked Pleskit.

"It's one of the most exciting events of the school year," said Ms. Weintraub enthusiastically. "Each of you will choose a topic to research. You do some experimenting, prepare a report, and even more important, some ways to demonstrate what you have learned. Then all of you bring your projects to the gym, and we all get to see what everyone has done."

"You could die from the thrills," muttered Jordan.

"I am sorry your metabolism is not sufficient to deal with the excitement," said Pleskit. "From my point of view, it sounds like fun."

Whoa! thought Tim. *Science fair meets alien technology. This could be too cool for words.*

This idea pleased him, since the science fair was usually an event filled with enormous pain and anxiety for Tim. It wasn't that he didn't like science; in fact, he loved it. But he could never manage to come up with a project as devastatingly cool as he truly wanted. Even worse, he had never once managed to get his project finished before two A.M. of the day that it was due.

"We'll pick our subjects next week and start serious work the week after that," said Ms. Weintraub.

The next couple of days were quiet. Tim and Pleskit talked every night on their new com-system, mostly discussing ways they could convince their parents to allow a sleepover. Ms. Weintraub distributed a list of suggestions for science fair projects. Homework was assigned. Tests were taken. Spitballs were thrown.

Then, on Friday afternoon, Brad Kent offered Pleskit a cookie.

Tim, who had been talking with Linnsy when it happened, saw the incident out of the corner of his eye. At first, it didn't register as anything suspicious. But even as he continued to talk, his brain began asking questions—questions such as:

Why is Jordan's official flunky and chief butt-kisser offering Pleskit a cookie?

Can this possibly be a good thing?

If not, why not?

And—the key question—what kind of cookies had Brad brought to school at least once a week every year since first grade?

The answers came rushing together in a moment of terror.

"Pleskit!" cried Tim. *Don't eat that cookie!*

It was too late.

Pleskit had eaten the cookie.

Another dose of peanut butter had just entered his bloodstream.

CHAPTER
11

Alien Romeo

Pleskit was slightly startled when Brad Kent offered him the cookie. However, he also knew that the sharing of food is one of the prime ways of building personal connections on almost every planet. So—wary, but not wanting to offend—he accepted the offer.

"Hmmm," he said, sniffing it. "A delectable aroma. Slightly familiar, and . . ." He closed his eyes and took a deeper breath. "Ah, yes. *Irresistible!*"

He took a large bite of the cookie, even as Tim cried out for him to stop and McNally lunged forward to grab it from him.

"What's the matter?" cried Pleskit, his *sphen-*

gnut-ksher emitting an odor unlike anything Tim had ever smelled before.

"Peanut butter!" cried Tim. "Pleskit, that's a peanut-butter cookie!"

Pleskit's eyes widened. The odor from his *sphen-gnut-ksher* changed to the now-familiar burning hair smell that indicated panic. He held the remainder of the cookie away from him, staring at it in horror.

McNally snatched it from his hand, sniffed it, took a bite. "That's peanut butter all right," he confirmed grimly.

"Gosh, Pleskit, I'm sorry," said Brad, trying desperately to control the smile twitching at the corners of his mouth. "I didn't even think about that."

Tim glanced to his side. Jordan was leaning against the building, holding his sides and squeezing his eyes shut as he tried to contain his laughter.

"You okay, Pleskit?" asked McNally.

Pleskit placed his hands on his stomach and closed his eyes. "I think I will be all right, O Guardian of My Well Being. I ate only one bite, and now that we know what to anticipate, I hope/expect I will be able to control my reaction. Even so, perhaps we should go inside for now."

"Good idea," said McNally.

As they left the playground, Tim stalked over to

Jordan and said angrily, "That was a rotten thing to do!"

"What?" cried Jordan, spreading his hands. "What did I do?" His eyes were wide with fake innocence, and he could barely get the words past his ongoing attempts to control his laughter.

"You know what I mean," snapped Tim. "You *told* Brad to give Pleskit that cookie!"

"Why, Tim," said Jordan soothingly. "I wouldn't do a thing like that to your little purple pal. Besides, it's not like I control Brad or anything. Anyway, that peanut-butter stuff is just an excuse Pleskit was using to get out of trouble. My father says its total baloney."

"It is not!" said Tim fiercely.

Jordan yawned in his face.

"It's chumps like you who give Earthlings a bad name!" snapped Tim. He turned to stalk away.

Jordan deftly stuck out one foot, tripped Tim, and sent him sprawling facedown in the dirt of the playground. "It's people like you who give clumsiness a bad name," he said mockingly.

"Maybe you should join Dweebs Anonymous," hooted Brad, who had slid over to stand beside Jordan.

Laughing uproariously, the two of them walked away.

* * *

73

When the class came back from recess, they found Pleskit sitting on top of his desk, leaning on one arm. "Why, Ms. Weintraub," he said smoothly. "You're looking sweeter than a *skibwee* today." A faint, flowery smell drifted from his *sphen-gnut-ksher*.

Ms. Weintraub blinked in surprise, then said firmly, "Pleskit, take your seat!"

Pleskit sighed but did as she asked. He rested his chin on his hands and stared at the teacher longingly—until Misty Longacres walked past him, at which point he turned and murmured, "Misty. Ah, Misty. A name like a poem. Was yours the face that stilled all hearts at *Kilgad-*

durr! Are those the hands that wove the *sheelkirk*'s robe?"

"Get down with that alien trash talk," snapped Misty.

"Don't mind me," murmured Pleskit. "It's part of an old poem from Hevi-Hevi. Have you ever thought about having purple children?"

Which was when Misty slapped his face.

"That's it!" cried McNally. Grabbing Pleskit by the arm, he hustled him out of the room.

Misty blinked, then looked at her hand, as if she couldn't believe what she had just done. "The aliens won't declare war over this, will they?" she murmured.

CHAPTER
12

The Accidental Spy

When Tim got home that afternoon, the alien message device was blinking. He turned it on and found a recording from Pleskit, complete with sight, sound, and smells.

"Tim," said Pleskit, his face serious. "Please call me as soon as you can. If you can come to the embassy, that would be even better." He burped twice, made a few knuckle cracks, and the picture vanished.

Tim scrawled a quick message to his mother, then grabbed his bike and headed for Thorncraft Park. The guard in the blue dome nodded when he saw him and said, "You're already cleared for entry, buddy." When Tim waited for him to open the dome, the guard added, "Hey, you still gotta press your palm to the wall so I can make sure it's really you and not some weird alien robot or something."

Tim did as the guard instructed. A few seconds later he was in the transport capsule. A few seconds after that he was inside the embassy.

He expected Pleskit to be waiting for him when the capsule opened, and was disappointed when he wasn't there. Then he remembered that he hadn't actually told Pleskit he was coming—had just hopped on his bike and ridden over. So he couldn't really expect Pleskit to be waiting for him. The guard must have announced him, though, for just moments later Pleskit came into the receiving area. He had the Veeblax with him. Tim could tell the little creature had been practicing its shapeshifting, because at the moment it looked like Pleskit's head—which made for a weird effect, since it was riding on his shoulder.

"What's up?" asked Tim. "Did your Fatherly One find out about school today?"

"Not yet," said Pleskit. "Though I am sure he will before long."

"It wasn't really your fault," said Tim reassuringly. "Brad gave you that cookie on purpose. And I'm positive Jordan was the one who set him up to do it."

"I figured as much," said Pleskit. His face got serious. The Veeblax imitated his expression. "I called because I want you to help me talk to the Fatherly One about all this."

"Geez, I dunno," said Tim. "Your Fatherly One is like this interplanetary big deal. He's not gonna listen to a kid like me. Besides, he's kind of scary."

"How do you think *I* feel about him?" asked Pleskit. "But it is a well-known phenomenon that Parental Units will accept information from their childling's friends that they will not accept from the childling itself. Please?"

Tim sighed. "He won't vaporize me if he gets mad, will he?"

Pleskit and the Veeblax shook their heads. "That is not the Fatherly One's way. Actually, if he does not like the idea that I asked you to speak on my behalf, the one most likely to suffer is me."

"Well, I don't want to get *you* in trouble, either," said Tim.

"I am in trouble already. Come on, let's go to the Fatherly One's office to wait for him."

When the boys reached Meenom's office, they were surprised to find no sign of anyone; not only was Meenom not there, but Ms. Buttsman, Barvgis, and Beezle Whompis were all missing as well.

"They must be having a staff meeting," said

Pleskit. "We'll go in and wait for him to come back."

"He might not like that," said Tim uneasily, remembering that the last time they had gone into Meenom's office, it had been to borrow his Molecule Compactor, something they had done without his permission.

"We're just going to wait for him," said Pleskit. "We won't touch anything."

Tim sighed and followed Pleskit into the office. Meenom's command pod floated halfway between the floor and the ceiling. Tim found himself having to press his hands against his sides to keep from reaching out and picking up any of the fascinating gadgets scattered around the office.

"*Zgribnick!*" said Pleskit suddenly. "I just remembered: the Fatherly One does not like me to bring the Veeblax in here. I'd better take him back."

"Wait!" said Tim.

"I'll be right back," said Pleskit, turning and walking backward as he spoke. "I need you to stay in case the Fatherly One comes. If he has not already heard about today's events, I want us to be the first to tell him." He turned again and hurried down the corridor.

Tim sighed. "I won't touch anything," he muttered to himself. "I won't touch anything. I won't touch anything. I *won't* touch anything."

79

He repeated the command to himself ten times before he broke down and picked up a strange-looking spherical object that kept changing color. As soon as he touched it, a smell like swamp water surrounded him. *Yikes!* thought Tim, moving quickly to set the thing back on the counter.

To his horror, he dropped it instead.

It rolled under the counter.

Diving to the floor, Tim began frantically looking for the little object.

Before he could spot it, he heard voices from the outer offices.

Swinging around on his knees, he saw Meenom standing in the outer office. He was talking to someone, but Tim couldn't see who. With a wave of his hand, Meenom turned and started toward the door.

Seized by terror, Tim scrambled under the counter and pressed himself against the wall.

As Pleskit was heading back to the Fatherly One's office to rejoin Tim, he was stopped in the hallway by Ms. Buttsman. "I don't think you should go disturb your Fatherly One right now," she said. "He has just received some unexpected visitors."

"But I need to speak to him!"

"It will have to wait. The visitors are from the

Interplanetary Trading Federation. Meenom gave strict orders that he is *not* to be interrupted."

"Off-worlders?" cried Pleskit.

"They arrived unexpectedly. They appeared to have very serious business."

Pleskit stared down the hall, wondering what would happen when his Fatherly One and three off-world visitors discovered an Earthboy in his office.

Even from his hiding place Tim could tell that the three beings who entered the office with Meenom were aliens. If their feet hadn't made it clear, their language would have. Cold with fear, he huddled even more tightly against the wall, praying that he wouldn't be discovered.

"Geedrill peedris fli-danji!" said one of the aliens in a voice that did not sound at all friendly.

Meenom burped loudly in response, then made a series of knuckle cracks. An odor that reminded Tim of a hamster cage that had gone too long without being changed filled the room. It was only his terror at being discovered that kept him from gagging out loud. He cupped his hand over his nose and tried to breathe shallowly, which helped, but not much.

A loud and frenzied conversation erupted among the aliens—a virtual symphony of words,

farts, belches, and knuckle cracks, accompanied by a series of smells so rich and varied they made Tim's head spin and his nostrils dizzy, which was not something he would have thought was possible.

What were the aliens talking about? And how angry would they be if they discovered he was listening?

Not that I've understood a single fart of it, thought Tim, wishing he had some idea—*any* idea—of what was going on.

A final burst of words and smells, and then the room fell silent, if not odor free. To Tim's horror, he saw Meenom's feet heading in his direction. He stopped in front of the shelf under which Tim was hiding. Speaking softly now, the ambassador picked up something and began to putter with it. As he did, he moved one foot forward.

It nudged against Tim.

Tim held his breath, trying not to make a sound.

Meenom dropped the object he had been holding—on purpose, Tim suspected.

He bent to pick it up, which brought him face to face with Tim. The boy cringed as he saw Meenom's eyes widen in shock and anger.

CHAPTER
13

Straight Talk

Tim had pushed himself as far back against the wall as he could, trying to merge himself into it. Now Meenom's purple face and dark eyes seemed to pin him to that spot. Unable to move, scarcely able to breathe, the boy mouthed a single word: *"Sorry!"*

To his astonishment, Meenom stood without speaking.

A moment later the aliens broke into another babble of conversation.

Feeling slightly less terrified, and driven by curiosity, Tim slid closer to the edge of his hiding place and peered out.

One of the aliens was clearly from Hevi-Hevi.

Another was tall and slender, with scaly orange skin. This being, whose back was toward Tim, wore little save a shiny brown cloth wrapped around its waist and a pair of brown shoes that fit so tightly it looked as if they had been painted on. Tim looked again and realized he could not tell if they really were shoes, or actually the creature's feet. The third being, who appeared to be female, had an insectlike quality to her features, especially her large, multifaceted eyes. She was waving her four arms and speaking in an angry, buzzing voice.

Meenom had his hands up and was humming a single, soft note, as if trying to calm her. A tangy-sweet odor, something like grapefruit, drifted from his *sphen-gnut-ksher*.

The conversation continued for another four or five minutes with the insect woman buzzing angrily, Meenom and the other Hevi-Hevian both trying to calm her, and the tall orange being occasionally adding a comment—which it seemed to do mostly by slapping out a rhythm on its skinny, scaly body.

A final, angry buzz from the insect woman was followed by a moment of silence. Then Meenom spoke, mingling words and gaseous eruptions in an oddly musical way. The insect woman buzzed two or three times during his reply, but other than that did not interrupt. When he was done she lowered her head and flicked out her tongue, which was about three feet long and bright blue. It wrapped around Meenom's wrist, then seemed to pull his hand and her head together. They stood that way for a moment. Then the insect woman withdrew her tongue, shook her head sadly, turned, and left the room. The tall orange alien followed. The third alien—the one from Hevi-Hevi—belched twice, emitted a smell that reminded Tim of root beer, patted Meenom on the shoulder, and turned to follow the others.

Meenom watched them go without speaking.

After they were gone, he belched a command. The door to the room slid shut.

He turned to where Tim was hiding and said sternly, "You can come out now."

Trying not to tremble, Tim crawled from beneath the shelf.

"What were you doing down there?" demanded Meenom.

Tim swallowed nervously. "Pleskit and I were waiting to talk to you. He left for a minute to . . . to do something. When I heard you coming, I freaked out and—"

Meenom raised a hand to stop him. "Freaked out?"

"Had a brain spasm," said Tim. "I thought you might get angry if you found me here by myself, so I hid. Maybe it was stupid, but I was really scared."

Meenom nodded. "I think I understand. My visitors, however, might not have. Having an Earthling here would have been . . . problematic for me. And for your planet. It does look a good deal like spying, you know."

"I'm just a kid!" said Tim desperately.

"Do you think children have never been used as spies before?" asked Meenom, sounding surprised.

"I suppose," said Tim. Then, feeling a need to get everything out, he added, "I did overhear the conversation. But you were all speaking in alien languages, so it's not like I really learned anything."

Meenom laughed. "A good point—though if you were working for one of my enemies, you could still have recorded the conversation to sell him later."

"I wouldn't do something like that!" cried Tim in horror. "I like you guys. Pleskit is my friend. I would never—"

"Peace, peace," said Meenom, holding out his hands. "I didn't say you were. I just pointed out the possibility." He burped twice and cracked his knuckles. The command pod drifted down to the floor. He stepped into it. "I am well aware that you have been a good, if not always wise, companion for Pleskit."

"I like him," said Tim. This answer had the double virtue of being true and seeming like a safe thing to say.

"He likes you as well, Tim. In fact, I am a bit envious of the friendship my childling shares with you. I do not have such an Earthling connection— nor am I likely to for some time. My work here is too serious, and too complicated, for me to make myself vulnerable in such a way. Yet such connections are, in the long run, one of the primary pleasures of the work. So it is a relief to speak with an Earthling who does not have an ax to grind or an economic interest to push." He paused, then said, "Tell me, how do you think Pleskit is adjusting?"

Tim, startled by the question—by the way Meenom was speaking to him—wasn't sure how to answer. "Good, I guess," he said. "Quite a bit better than I would, probably, now that I think about it."

The discussion had made Tim remember his first experience at summer camp two years earlier, and the desperate homesickness that had gripped him for the first few days. That had been in a place where the land, the sky, the trees, the air, the very beings around him were, if not what he saw every day, at least familiar and safe. As if a curtain had been pulled back, he suddenly had a new sense of what it was like for Pleskit to be here in this totally new place, where nothing was like what he was used to, where everyone he went to school with was of a completely different species. He blinked, stunned by this sudden vision of what his friend had been going through. Looking at Meenom more closely, he asked, "Does he talk about it much?"

"Not as much as I would like. On the other hand, I am not available to him as much as I would like to be. Things right now are . . . busy. And difficult."

Feeling bold, and thinking he might never have another chance, Tim said, "Were those beings that were just here giving you trouble?"

Meenom emitted a smell that reminded Tim of overripe bananas. "They were *messengers* of trouble."

"Do you have a lot of alien visitors?" asked Tim.

"I prefer the term off-worlders," said Meenom gently. "It's a little less harsh."

"Sorry."

Meenom burped reassuringly. "You don't know unless I tell you. And no, we have not had many off-world visitors. Earth is not on any of the major interplanetary lanes, so ships do not pass nearby very often. The beings who were just here came out of their way to express their concerns." He closed his eyes for a moment. "There are great forces moving, Tim. I am in a constant state of fret. I must be wise and wary if I am to protect your planet."

"Protect us?" asked Tim nervously.

Meenom looked startled. "Forgive me. I have spoken more freely than I should. It is not right to burden you with my concerns. Let us stay with Pleskit. This last . . . episode . . . of his has created new problems with the Trading Federation."

"But it wasn't really his fault," said Tim uneasily, wondering if Meenom had even heard about *today's* problem yet.

Meenom cracked his knuckles and emitted a faint fishy odor. "I wish I could be sure of that. I do not always understand my childling, especially after the events that occurred on our last planet, Geembol Seven."

"What happened there?" asked Tim eagerly.

Meenom tapped his nose three times. "I have said too much. I will ask you to keep this conversation in confidence. It might disturb Pleskit to know I was talking to you this way."

"I guess I can do that," said Tim uneasily. He started to say more but was interrupted by Ms. Buttsman rushing into the room. "Sir, I think you had better come quickly. We've got more trouble!"

CHAPTER
14

Grand Delusions

Tim and Meenom rushed out of his private office, into the area where Beezle Whompis had his desk.

The alien delegation was still there. The reason they had not left was clear: Pleskit had thrown himself to the floor and was clutching the insect-like woman around her ankles.

"Don't leave me," he pleaded desperately. "We could make beautiful music together. I love the way you click, baby."

"Good grief," muttered Tim. "He's having a peanut-butter flashback!"

"Pleskit!" roared Meenom. "What do you think you're doing?"

"Following my heart, O Fatherly One, just as

you have always taught me to do. I have finally found the woman of my dreams. I cannot let her simply blast off and leave me!"

The insect woman made a series of angry-sounding clicks and chitters as she tried to shake Pleskit away.

"Pleskit, stand up this minute!" roared Meenom. The smell that accompanied his command nearly knocked Tim over.

Pleskit blinked and leaped to his feet. "Save me from myself!" he cried.

Then he ran from the room.

The visiting aliens all spoke at once, none of them using words that Tim could understand. Meenom hurried forward, belching soothingly.

Tim scurried around the group and took off after Pleskit.

He was in his room, huddled on his air mattress. (Since the mattress was made of nothing but specially treated air, he looked as if he were floating about a foot off the floor.)

"I am not fit to live among civilized beings," groaned Pleskit.

"That's okay," said Tim, trying to sound cheerful. "At least you'll still fit in here on Earth!"

"There is no humor in this, Tim. I am a walking disgrace, an embarrassment waiting to happen, a social disaster area, a scandal on—"

"All right, all right! I get the picture. But that was just another peanut-butter episode, right?"

"I do not know," groaned Pleskit. "I don't know anything anymore."

Later that afternoon Meenom called Pleskit into his office.

"What, exactly, is going on with you?" asked the Fatherly One sternly. "In addition to that outrageous episode with our guest from Peablam VI, the school has called to complain of yet another episode in the classroom."

"I think we have isolated the source of the problem," said Pleskit eagerly. "I seem to have an extreme reaction to an Earthling food called peanut butter."

Meenom's *sphen-gnut-ksher* sparked, never a good sign. "We are both well aware that new elements in your environment may disturb your metabolism. However, you have been trained from hatching to control yourself better than this. Pleskit, there is too much at stake right now. If you can't keep yourself under control, I fear I will have to withdraw you from the school."

"But, Fatherly One—"

"No more!" said Meenom, raising his hands to cut off Pleskit's protest. "Please, do not add to my already considerable problems."

His insides cold and heavy, Pleskit trudged from the office back to his room.

Things did not improve any the next morning. When Pleskit and McNally arrived at school, they found a new crowd of protesters and picketers, most of them carrying signs that said things like KEEP OUR CHILDREN SAFE and ALIEN HARASSMENT MUST STOP and WOULD YOU SEND YOUR DAUGHTER TO THIS SCHOOL?

Mr. Grand again called Pleskit to the office.

"Your presence here is beginning to affect the other students," he said sadly. "While I am personally fond of you, Pleskit, I cannot let your problems in self-control affect the educational program I am trying to run. I'm sure you understand that this cannot go on."

"I completely agree," said Pleskit.

"Good," said Mr. Grand. "So I know you will not take it the wrong way when I tell you that I have sent a message to your Parental Unit suggesting that he withdraw you from the school, for the good of yourself, the other students, and the developing interplanetary relationship."

"You're throwing me out?" cried Pleskit in horror.

Mr. Grand frowned. "That's a very harsh way to phrase it, Pleskit. I am suggesting a voluntary withdrawal, for the sake of all concerned."

"But it's not my—"

"Ah-ah!" said Mr. Grand. "I don't want to hear any excuses. It's time for you to stop blaming your behavior on some 'chemical reaction' and start accepting responsibility for your own actions. Chemistry only counts in chemistry class."

That afternoon Pleskit asked Tim to come to the embassy with him again.

"I do not know what to do," Pleskit said, once they were in the privacy of his room. "The Fatherly One has been called away to urgent meetings, all of which seem to have to do with the disruption I have caused. The good news is, that means he has not yet received Mr. Grand's message asking that I be taken out of school. The bad news is, he will get that message shortly after he returns." He flung himself onto the air mattress. "I despair, Tim. It seems I bring trouble everywhere I go."

"I can't believe that guy!" said Tim angrily. "He's just doing this because you're an alien. If you were an Earth kid he'd have to go through all kinds of stuff before he could kick you out. You can tell how hard it is to throw a kid out just by the fact that we still have Jordan in our midst." He paused in his rant. "How about McNally? Have you talked to him about this?"

"Of course. He says that if the problem were

how to get a girl interested, he could help me. He seems to feel that is one of his specialties. But on the matter of getting *un*interested in girls, he is of no use."

"Hmmm. We can't count on the Butt for help; she would just as soon have you out of the school anyway. What about Beezle Whompis?"

Pleskit looked up in surprise. "I had not thought about him. I do not really know him yet. He is a very strange being."

"Yeah," laughed Tim. "Not normal, like us."

"He does not even have a regular body," said Pleskit.

"That might make him all the more suited to discuss bodily functions," said Tim. "He can take an outsider's view on the question."

When the boys entered the outer office, where Beezle Whompis normally held guard over Meenom's door, they were disappointed to see that the new secretary was not at his desk.

They were turning to go when they heard a crackle of sound. Suddenly Beezle Whompis was there.

"Sorry," he said. "It takes a fair amount of energy to maintain my physical appearance. Sometimes I let it slip when no one is around, just to rest for a bit. Can I help you, Pleskit?"

Quickly Pleskit explained what had happened

with Mr. Grand at school that day. Beezle Whompis's long, lean face grew dark with anger. He shimmered out of sight and reappeared next to Pleskit. "It is not appropriate for a man charged with the education of children to have such a slight understanding of the way chemistry affects the brain, of the way body and mind are linked together. The same kind of thing that happened to you could easily happen to a human, given the right foodstuff."

"You mean you could make humans fall in love that way?" asked Tim nervously.

"Not necessarily that specific reaction," said Beezle Whompis. "I just mean that you could create a short-term personality change." He peered at Tim more closely. "You look skeptical, young Earthling. Perhaps a demonstration is in order."

"You mean you've got something like that already?" asked Tim.

Beezle Whompis smiled. "Of course not. But I suspect I could work something up without much trouble." He paused for a moment and went frizzy around the edges. Then, as if he had made up his mind about something, he grew solid again and said, "Follow me."

The air crackled as he vanished from sight. A moment later he reappeared. "Sorry! I keep forgetting that you physical creatures have to travel with your bodies intact. Let's try that again."

He led them to another level of the embassy, then along a corridor Tim had not seen before. They came to a door marked with a set of alien symbols. Tim's heart sank. Underneath the symbols was a plaque that said, in English, RESTRICTED ACCESS: NO EARTHLINGS ALLOWED!

The phrase was repeated—at least, Tim assumed it was the same phrase—in French, Spanish, and several other languages that he recognized as Earthly but could not name.

Beside the door was something that looked like a keypad. On its surface were fifteen buttons, each of a different color.

Tim expected Beezle Whompis to tap in a code. Instead, the tall, cadaverous alien pointed a single long finger at the keypad.

A crackle of energy shot from his fingertip to the pad.

The door slid open.

CHAPTER
15

Monkeyfood

When Beezle Whompis noticed Tim hanging back, he laughed and said, "Feel free to enter."

Tim still hung back. "I don't want to get you in trouble," he said. "And the sign said 'No Earthlings Allowed.' "

Beezle Whompis made a sound like a car trying to start on a freezing cold morning. (It wasn't until later that Tim learned this was his way of laughing.) Reaching forward, the energy being tapped him on the head and said, "There. I have just granted you temporary galactic citizenship." He paused, then added, "Actually, I believe you are the first Earthling to be so honored—at least, by this mission."

TRANSLATION:
ENGLISH

HUMANOID
'DNA'
COMPRISED OF
2% CULTURED, CIVILISED,
INTELLIGENT MATERIAL.
ILL-MANNERED PRIMEVAL
98% PRIMATE MATERIAL.

"Cool," said Tim. "Thanks!"

He followed Beezle Whompis and Pleskit into the room. "Cool," he murmured again, lost in awe at the sight of all the alien scientific equipment. Two long tables that looked as if they were made of blue glass held everything from bottles and beakers to conglomerations of wire and plastic that were so complicated it made Tim's eyes hurt to try to figure them out. Viewscreens and monitors lined one wall. He saw three workstations; each had a chair with keypads on the arms and additional keypads in front of it.

Beezle Whompis sizzled out of sight and reappeared in one of the chairs. Rather than tapping any of the keys, he placed a finger against a lavender button. For a moment he seemed to fade. A blue glow flickered around him.

"Ah," he said. "There we go."

A flood of symbols filled the viewscreen in front of Beezle Whompis.

"What is that?" asked Tim.

"A complete map of the human genome. Everything you ever wanted to know about your own DNA but didn't know how to ask."

Tim gulped. "You just have it on file? The government is spending, like, billions of dollars to come up with that information."

"The exercise will be good for them," muttered

Beezle Whompis, his attention focused on the screen. "Ah, here we go! Hmmm. Oh, *that's* interesting." He began to chuckle. Then he flickered blue again. The screen changed. "Good," said the energy being softly. "Good. Good. *Aha!* I think we've got it."

Crackling out of sight, he reappeared again next to the door. "Let's go to the kitchen. I want to see if Shhh-foop can whip up a little recipe for us. Tim, if you're willing to taste it, the results should be . . . amusing."

When they reached the kitchen, they found that Beezle Whompis's "recipe" had already been transferred to Shhh-foop's computer terminal.

"Oh, yes, making this will be lovely fun," she sang, her orange tentacles whirling excitedly. "Sit right down, younglings and Mr. Whompis, and I'll get to work. Would you like a snack while you wait?"

"Uh—I think one special food will be enough for me today," said Tim.

"Alas, alas," warbled Shhh-foop. "Young Earthlings fear the cooking of Shhh-foop. Where is the spirit of adventure? Gone, gone . . ."

Since she sang it more to herself than to him, Tim didn't feel it was necessary to answer.

"I'd like a bowl of *febril gnurxis*," said Pleskit.

This was his favorite breakfast cereal, but sometimes he had it for an after-school snack.

Beezil Whompis vanished altogether. When he reappeared, he explained to Tim, "Having no actual physical body to nourish, I sustain myself by snacking on energy. Sometimes I go outside to bathe in the sunshine. This time I simply slipped into the embassy's circuits for a little electron soup, so to speak."

"Ready!" sang Shhh-foop a few minutes later. She slid over to the table, holding a silvery tray. On the tray were a stack of crackers (or something that looked like crackers), a spreader, and a bowl of goo. The goo actually looked a little like peanut butter, or at least like peanut butter would look if it were purple, not quite as thick, and given to releasing an occasional bubble, almost like a glass of soda working in slow motion. Or lava.

To Tim's surprise, the stuff *smelled* amazingly good.

"What is it?" he asked.

Beezle Whompis smiled. "Try it and see."

"I haven't had real good luck with alien food," said Tim nervously, remembering the explosive aftereffects of the *finnikle-pokta* he had eaten the first time he visited the embassy.

"Ah, but this is designed to be compatible with

the human digestive system," said Beezle Whompis soothingly.

Tim took a deep breath, then reached forward and spread some of the goo on one of the cracker things.

The smell was so delicious that he found he was actually eager to eat it.

He took a bite, then chewed for a minute.

"Good!" he cried, popping the rest of the cracker into his mouth. "*Very* good!"

He spread another and ate it. Beezle Whompis stopped him as he was reaching for the third.

"Let's wait and see what happens," he said.

Tim looked longingly at the bowl of goo. "Okay," he sighed. "But I want Shhh-foop to give that recipe to my mom."

"Actually, I doubt your mother will want this one," said Beezle Whompis.

Tim started to answer. Before he could get the words out of his mouth, his eyes went wide. He twitched twice.

"Oook!" He said, scratching under his arm. "OOO-OO-O-OK!"

Then he leaped from his chair. Leaning forward, he pressed his hands against the floor like an extra pair of feet, then went scrambling out of the room.

"*Ai-yi-yikkle-demonga!*" wailed Shhh-foop, forgetting, for the first time since the embassy had landed, Meenom's rule about speaking in the language of the host country. She sounded like an opera singer losing her mind.

Beezle Whompis crackled out of sight. Pleskit sprinted down the hall after his friend, wondering in horror if his Fatherly One's new assistant was a traitor like Mikta-makta-mookta after all.

CHAPTER
16

Monkey Business

Pleskit found Tim leaping up and down on top of
Ms. Buttsman's desk, shrieking "Ook! Ook!" as
he flung papers into the air.

Ms. Buttsman, crouched underneath the desk,
was shrieking for help.

"Tim!" cried Pleskit sternly. "Tim, get down
from there!"

"AAAAIIEEEE!" cried Ms. Buttsman, which
didn't really help things much.

"Oook!" said Tim. Then he vaulted off the desk
and raced across the room, where he began trying
to climb one of the embassy's plants. The plant's
large purple leaves whirled wildly as it tried to de-
fend itself from the intruder. It was just reaching

out with a wiry purple vine when Tim leaped away and onto one of the seating devices.

Pleskit took several deep breaths, trying to keep himself from slipping into *kleptra.* Ms. Buttsman peered over the edge of the desk and shrieked again.

At that moment Beezle Whompis crackled into view. "This way, McNally," he called behind him. "Hurry!"

An instant later McNally appeared at the door of the room.

"Oook! Oook!" squealed Tim.

McNally heaved a deep sigh and strode to the seating device where Tim was hunched. "Tim, get down from there!" he said sharply.

Tim leaped forward, landed on McNally's shoulder, then scrambled over him and leaped to the floor. With another "oook!" he headed for the door.

McNally made a flying tackle and caught him just before he left the room.

"Well," said Beezle Whompis triumphantly. "I guess that proves the point!"

"Oook!" shrieked Tim.

"Do you have an antidote?" asked Pleskit nervously.

"Only time," said Beezle Whompis. "Another ten minutes or so and he should be fine."

"Easy for you to say," growled McNally, who was struggling to keep Tim from crawling away from him. "What did you do to the kid anyway?"

"Just gave him a little monkeyfood," said Beezle Whompis, sounding so innocent it was actually possible to believe he didn't see anything wrong in the idea.

"What," demanded Ms. Buttsman, crawling out from under her desk, "are you talking about?" She began fussing with her hair.

"Just a small experiment, dear lady," said Beezle Whompis, causing Ms. Buttsman to snort in disdain. "We wanted to see if we could create a re-action in Tim similar to what peanut butter causes in Pleskit. The substance we came up with stimulated what your scientists sometimes refer to as 'the lizard brain,' causing Tim to revert to a primitive, apelike behavior that lies hidden as a latent possibility in every human."

"Given that boy's typical behavior, I don't think getting him to act like an ape represents any great scientific breakthrough," said Ms. Buttsman scornfully.

"I believe the ambassador prefers the staff not to say insulting things about our host species," replied Beezle Whompis smoothly.

Ms. Buttsman snorted again and started to gather the papers Tim had strewn about. "I'll thank you to remove him until . . . until whatever it is you did wears off," she said. Her voice was so cold you could have cut up the words and used them in a drink.

Beezle Whompis nodded to McNally, who managed to pick up the still-ooking Tim and carry him from the room.

Beezle Whompis's prediction turned out to be completely correct. In ten minutes' time Tim reverted to his normal self. Blinking, he looked at McNally and said, "Why are you holding me?"

"Let *them* explain," growled McNally. "I'm supposed to be on break right now!" Letting go of Tim, he began brushing off his clothes. "He all right now?" he asked Beezle Whompis.

"He should be fine."

"Good. Next time you try an experiment like this, you might tie him down first. Or at least do it while I'm not taking my nap."

Shaking his head, he left the room.

Pleskit quickly explained to Tim what had happened after he ate the substance Shhh-foop had prepared.

"Wow!" said Tim. "It really is monkeyfood! Now Mr. Grand will have to believe us!"

Mr. Grand, of course, did no such thing. When the boys went to see him the next day he listened to their story with growing annoyance.

"A fine concoction," he said when they were finished. He began pacing back and forth in front of them with his hands clasped behind his back. "If you boys were doing this for a creative writing project, I would expect you to get a good grade. But you don't need to be telling *me* this kind of fairy tale. I don't believe in such nonsense. People control their own destiny, and there is no sense blaming their actions on chemicals. That is the coward's way out—all excuses and no accountability. A real man takes responsibility for his actions."

Mrs. Vanderhof was outraged on their behalf. "I can't believe that man is so obdurate!" she fumed, setting a plate of chocolate chip cookies on the table in front of Linnsy, Pleskit, and Tim. "Of course people should be responsible for their own behavior. But it's not always possible. He's so stuck on that one idea that he's ignoring reality!"

Pleskit glanced at the cookies. "Do these have any peanut butter in them?" he asked nervously.

Mrs. Vanderhof looked offended. Then her face relaxed. "You're smart to be cautious, dear. But no, there's no peanut butter in them. I made them for the PTA Welcome Back event tonight." She smiled. "I figured I ought to have you three sample them first—to make sure they're good enough."

"Good figuring!" said Tim enthusiastically.

Still looking a little nervous, Pleskit picked up a cookie and took a big bite. *"Skeegil sprixis!"* he cried. "These are wonderful!"

Mrs. Vanderhof smiled modestly. The smile faded as her thoughts returned to Mr. Grand. "That man makes me so angry! Even if he doesn't trust my experience—or yours, Pleskit—he really ought to know that three kids in your very class are taking Ritalin to control their behavior."

"They are?" said Linnsy, at the same time that Pleskit asked, "What's Ritalin?"

Mrs. Vanderhof looked a little uncomfortable. "It's a drug that helps some people focus better. Some kids who have trouble concentrating find it helps their behavior in school considerably."

"Who's taking it?" asked Tim eagerly.

Mrs. Vanderhof shook her head. "That's not my story to tell. You know I believe in being completely open about what I've experienced, Tim. But I also believe other people have to make that decision for themselves. The point is, your principal has proof right in his classrooms of the way body chemistry affects behavior, and he should be aware of it."

"Proof or not, he's still threatening to ask Meenom to pull Pleskit out of school," said Tim bitterly.

"He hasn't done it already?" asked Mrs. Vanderhof.

"The Fatherly One is not always easy to get in touch with," Pleskit explained. "He has been traveling for the last couple of days. But he is coming home this evening, and I fear he may want to go to the PTA reception. If he does, Mr. Grand will almost certainly talk to him while he's there, since he knows he may not get another chance right away."

"Then we have to do something tonight," said Linnsy. "It's our last chance!"

"Do *what?*" asked Pleskit.

She shrugged. "I don't know. A demonstration or something. Prove to Grand the monkeyfood does what you said. Then he'll have to accept the idea that the peanut butter could have caused your troubles."

Tim put down his cookie and sighed. "Well, I guess there's no way around it. I'm going to have to make a monkey out of myself again—this time in public!"

CHAPTER
17

Swinging Party

The Parent-Teacher Association usually held its annual Welcome Back Night earlier in the school year. But the disruption—and security problems—caused by having the world's first alien in attendance had caused the group to move the date back to early October.

Some parents grumbled about the armed guards, and having to come through two sets of scanners before being allowed into the school. Others said they thought *every* school should have such an elaborate security system. Others were grumpy about the protesters, who were still standing just outside the police lines, and shouting anti-alien slogans at the people who were allowed in.

Because Tim's mother had been scheduled for a late shift at the hospital where she worked, and hadn't been able to get out of it, Tim came with Linnsy and her parents. Given what he was planning to do that night, this was just as well as far as he was concerned, even though he did find Linnsy's father somewhat frightening.

"Well, doesn't this look nice!" said Mrs. Vanderhof when they came in.

The cafeteria had been decorated with artwork from most of the classes and a big WELCOME BACK banner made by the fourth graders stretched across the back wall.

Tim looked around, wondering if Pleskit had arrived yet.

At the embassy, Pleskit had been getting more and more nervous as the time for the PTA event drew closer. The Fatherly One had called in three times, saying he hoped to arrive home in time to attend but that if he was not there by seven that Pleskit and McNally should go without him, and he would catch up with them later if he could.

It usually bothered Pleskit that his Fatherly One missed so many school events. This time, however, he was very glad for the delay. He had Shhh-foop prepare another batch of monkeyfood for him, which they stored in a small plastic container.

At 7:05, he and McNally left for the school.

"Look, there he is!"

"It's the alien boy!"

"Holy cow, he really *is* purple!"

Whispers like this rustled through the crowd when Pleskit and McNally entered the cafeteria. Parents who had not yet had a chance to see the alien in person were elbowing to get near him. Everywhere people were craning their necks to see the world's most famous sixth-grader.

It took Tim several minutes to work his way through the crowd to his friend's side, and he had to step on a fair number of toes in the process.

"Have you got the goo?" he whispered, when he finally reached his goal.

"Right here," said Pleskit, patting the pocket that held the container he and Shhh-foop had prepared.

"Then Operation Monkey is underway," said Tim, feeling highly pleased with himself.

Only it wasn't, really. As they watched for their opportunity, they realized the flaw in their plan: Mr. Grand was spending almost all his time talking to the adults, and wasn't going to be particularly interested in talking to any kids—

particularly kids he viewed as trouble—on this occasion.

"Now what do we do?" muttered Tim.

"Let's try standing by the food table," suggested Pleskit. "I've noticed that Mr. Grand has what you call a 'sweet tooth.' He's bound to come that way sooner or later."

"What are you two plotting now?" asked McNally, when he saw them whispering.

"Just going for cookies," said Pleskit. "Want to come?"

"As if I had a choice," muttered McNally. "Stand back, everyone!" he bellowed. "Coming through. Give the kid some air."

Tim was astonished at how much easier it was to move through the room with McNally in the lead.

Mrs. Vanderhof was standing behind the food table, smiling and chatting as she poured glasses of punch and helped people find just the right cookie. "Any luck, boys?" she asked when she saw Tim and Pleskit standing in front of her.

"Not so far," said Tim glumly.

"We thought if we waited here, we might have a better chance of talking to him," said Pleskit.

"Good plan," said Linnsy. She had just come out of the kitchen with a new platter of cookies. "Mr. Grand always chows down hard at these things."

"These two all right with you for a minute, Ma'am?" asked McNally.

"Of course," said Mrs. Vanderhof with a smile.

"All right, don't move," said McNally to Pleskit. "I'll be back in a minute."

He poured two glasses of punch, and began to make his way through the crowd again. To Tim's surprise, he was heading for Ms. Weintraub. Tim was even more surprised by the way their teacher smiled when McNally handed her the glass of punch. But before he had time to think about that, he saw Mr. Grand coming toward them.

His throat got dry. Somehow he found the idea of speaking to the principal—who was already unhappy with him—far more unnerving than any of the very real dangers he and Pleskit had faced since they first met each other.

He waited till Mr. Grand was nearly at the table.

"Could I have a word with you, sir?" he asked, trying hard to sound polite. "It's about Pleskit."

Mr. Grand frowned. "This is not the time for anything like that, Tim. Come see me tomorrow."

"But tomorrow will be—"

He didn't bother to finish the sentence. Mr. Grand had turned and left.

"This isn't going to work after all!" groaned Tim. "He's not going to give us a chance!"

"On Hevi-Hevi," replied Pleskit, "we say, 'If the

pawpreet won't come to the *skrizzle,* the *skrizzle* must go to the *pawpreet.*' "

Tim scowled. "What the heck does that mean?"

Pleskit pointed to the front of the room, where a microphone had been set on the stage for short speeches from Mr. Grand and the PTA officers.

Tim gulped. He had been ready to make a fool of himself in public in order to help Pleskit, but he hadn't really counted on doing it *onstage.*

"If Mr. Grand's request that I be pulled from the school reaches the Fatherly One, the humiliation will be unbearable," said Pleskit. "However, that is not my deepest worry. If he files a formal request for withdrawal with the embassy, it will have to be passed on to higher levels. It could be deadly for the Fatherly One's mission!"

Tim took a deep breath. "Give me the monkey-food," he said. "I have a duty to Earth!"

Taking the container from Pleskit's outstretched hand, Tim began to work his way to the front of the cafeteria.

CHAPTER
18

Monkeyfood Mania

As Tim got closer to the stage his stomach began to get tighter and tighter.

What am I doing? part of his brain was shrieking.

He was getting two answers. One section of his brain was boldly saying, *You are saving the mission, helping your friend, and protecting the entire planet.* Another, milder part of his brain was saying, *What are you doing? Making an incredible fool of yourself, that's what you're doing!*

Tim hated making a fool of himself. On the other hand, he was used to it.

And the stakes were high.

A set of six steps led up to the stage. Tim

climbed them, feeling as if he were mounting the gallows. At first only a few people noticed him, since almost everyone was busy in conversation.

He went to the microphone and turned it on.

"Ladies and gentlemen," he said.

His words came out even louder than he had expected. Conversations began to die down. People turned in his direction. Some people looked puzzled, but it was obvious that most of them thought he was part of the program.

He looked out on the sea of faces and was horrified to see Jordan Lynch and Brad Kent standing near the edge of the stage. He hadn't even thought about them being here. He felt himself begin to blush.

Too late to turn back now, he thought. Tightening his grip on the microphone stand, he said, "As some of you may know, my friend Pleskit has had some . . . uh . . . problems of a romantic nature recently."

Everyone was looking at him now.

"The thing is, all that wasn't really Pleskit's fault. See, it turns out he has this, like, allergy to peanut butter, and when he eats it, it just makes him go kind of girl crazy."

To Tim's horror, he saw Mr. Grand pushing his way through the crowd, a furious look on his face.

He began to talk faster. "The problem is, some people don't really believe that's what was happening. Some people insist that blood chemistry can't affect your behavior at all. So we needed to give you some proof." He held up the jar of monkeyfood. "Here it is. This is a food we cooked up over at the embassy. I'm going to eat some now, and you'll see how it causes me to act like a monkey."

"That's enough, Tim!" shouted Mr. Grand. He was almost at the stage now.

Tim tried to open the monkeyfood. To his horror, the top wouldn't come off the container!

Mr. Grand was at the edge of the stage.

"The bottom!" shouted Pleskit from the far side of the room. "Push on the bottom, Tim!"

Tim pushed the bottom. The top of the container popped open. He was about to stick in his finger and take a swipe of the goo when Mr. Grand stormed up beside him and snatched the container from his hand.

"Tim, how foolish do you think I am?" he said angrily. "You can eat this food and then pretend to act like a monkey, and what does it prove? Nothing but that you wanted to act like a monkey."

"He acts like a monkey anyway!" shouted Jordan, who was obviously enjoying this.

"Quiet!" snapped Mr. Grand. "Now look, this

is utter nonsense, and I'm going to prove it once and for all."

To Tim's horror the principal stuck one finger into the container, took out a big gob of purple goo, then stuck his finger into his mouth and licked it off.

"There!" he said. "Now if there was anything at all to this nonsense you've been spout—"

Mr. Grand stopped. He clutched at his throat. His face twitched. His eyes went wide.

"Oook!" he cried, bending forward and scratching himself under his arm. "Oook! Oook!"

Most people in the cafeteria looked baffled. A few, assuming it was some sort of skit, began to laugh. Others looked frightened.

"Aoooga!" cried Mr. Grand, pounding his chest and stomping across the stage. "A-*oooo*-ga!"

Now people began to look really nervous. Someone screamed. Several parents grabbed their kids and ran for the exits. A few ran for the exits without their kids. Tim noticed Jordan scrambling under one of the tables.

"Aoooga!" cried Mr. Grand again. He grabbed the microphone and began snorting into it, then shrieked and pounded the microphone against the floor.

Mr. Philgrinn, the gym teacher, rushed toward the stage. Five of the fathers joined him.

Seeing them coming, Mr. Grand leaped across the stage, grabbed the edge of the curtain, and began to climb. When he reached the top he flung himself over their heads onto one of the cafeteria tables.

"Aoooga!" he cried, pounding his chest. "Aoooga!"

Three more parents—two mothers and a father—tried to grab him.

Flexing his legs, he leaped straight up and grabbed one of the support beams that stretched across the cafeteria ceiling. Swinging from beam to beam, he began making his way toward the refreshment tables.

Shrieking people scrambled to get out of his way.

He landed on the end of the table—the *very* end, which made it act like a huge lever.

Mr. Grand's end of the table went down.

The other end went up.

Cookies, cakes, and cups of punch soared across the room.

That was when McNally made a flying tackle and dropped him.

Tim wasn't sure whether to laugh or run for his life.

Then he looked to the side of the room and saw Pleskit's Fatherly One standing in the cafeteria doorway.

Running had definitely been the right answer.

Unfortunately, it was too late for that.

CHAPTER
19

Final Test

Pleskit's Fatherly One was not happy. He had been not happy when he nabbed the boys at the PTA reception. He had been not happy during the drive back to the embassy in the limousine. And he had been not happy as he led them to his office.

Now, pacing back and forth in front of his command pod, he was still not happy.

"That was totally irresponsible," he fumed. His *sphen-gnut-ksher* was emitting the smell of disapproval, which reminded Tim of insect repellent with a slight overtone of burnt toast.

"It was also totally undignified," said Ms. Buttsman.

"Thank you for your input, Ms. Buttsman,"

said Meenom. "Would you please fetch Mr. Mc-Nally for me?"

Ms. Buttsman gave him a sour look but went to do as he asked. Once she had gone from the room, Meenom said, "Now, much as I disapprove of what you did, I must admit that you got your point across rather clearly. I have already received a call from Mr. Grand saying that if we will fully explain to the press what prompted his eruption of monkey-behavior tonight, he will withdraw his objections to your remaining at the school, take any reference to past problems out of your permanent record, and replace them with a note saying you should not be allowed to consume peanut butter in any form, as it affects your brain chemistry."

He paused, then added, "I fear I did not give you sufficient credit for your story of what had happened to you, Pleskit. You have my apology."

Pleskit nodded. "Accepted, O Fatherly One."

Meenom raised an eyebrow, made a clicking sound at the corner of his mouth, and emitted a smell like lemon juice. "Don't get carried away. You're still in plenty of trouble. As are you, Timothy."

Tim blushed and looked nervous.

"We will determine what discipline you will receive later," said Meenom. "Tim's, of course, will come from his own Parental Unit. Right now, however, I wish to move on to other matters—namely, the issue of peanut butter. Do we have any in the embassy?"

"I do not believe so, Fatherly One."

"Actually, we do," said McNally, who had just entered the room. "I keep a jar myself. For snacking purposes, you know."

"Would you bring me some, Mr. McNally? I would like to conduct a brief experiment."

McNally raised an eyebrow, then shrugged and said, "Be right back."

The boys watched eagerly as Meenom opened the jar of peanut butter, held it beneath his nose, and sniffed.

"Divine aroma," he said. Then he dipped one long, purple finger into the peanut butter, took out a good-sized dollop, and popped it into his mouth. "Mmmm! A strange taste, but most excellent. You say this is a common food on your planet, Tim?"

"I eat it every day."

At that moment Ms. Buttsman entered the room. "Sir, I have a message for you from—"

She broke off as Meenom leaped to his feet. "Ms. Buttsman! Has anyone ever told you what a gorgeous creature you are? The sunsets of

Brikzanti are as nothing compared to your eyes."
Climbing onto his desk, he clasped his hands over
his heart and cried, "I must have you or die!"

Ms. Buttsman shrieked and ran from the room.

Meenom blinked, shook his head, and took a
deep breath. He stared at the jar of peanut butter
in wonder.

Then he began to laugh.

"What?" cried Pleskit. "What is so funny, O
Fatherly One?"

"This is it!" said Meenom, his *sphen-gnut-ksher* emitting the floral scent of triumph. "Our
first export, Pleskit! We can sell tons of this stuff
on Hevi-Hevi. We'll call it 'Return to Romance.' It
will be a public service!"

Bowing to Tim and Pleskit, he said, "My thanks
to you both. You have saved the mission!"

A Letter Home

FROM: Pleskit Meenom, on the always-interesting Planet Earth
TO: Maktel Geebrit, on the much-missed Planet Hevi-Hevi

Dear Maktel:

Well, that's it—the story of the strange new substance that you'll probably be hearing about as soon as the new selling campaign is ready. I hope Hevi-Hevi is ready for all that romance!

The Fatherly One and I have discussed the new export in some detail. He says that civilization requires the control of our own urges, which in many cases means understanding and conquering our own chemistry. But to conquer chemistry, we must first acknowledge it. If we pretend it does not count, then we can never deal with the reality of how it affects us.

Anyway, I hope you got a kick out of hearing about my latest problem. Though I worked closely with the writer guy, it felt strange to let someone else tell the story. If anything else happens—which, given my life here so far, seems inevitable—I may tell you about it myself. I'm not sure I liked sharing all my secret feelings with the writer guy.

Actually, I did not tell him *all* my secret feelings. Though I was completely honest, there were a couple of things I kept to myself, partly because I have learned that Earthlings are often uncomfortable talking about emotions. I didn't say anything about how homesick I get, for example, or how strange this world seems to me from day to day as I try to get used to it, how I long for the familiar sights and smells of Hevi-Hevi. Sometimes I feel so far from home that it is like a big lump has grown in my *clinkus* and I can hardly move.

It's not as if I am totally alone. I have been making friends here. I have the Fatherly One, and the Grandfatherly One. Most of all, I have Tim. I didn't really talk about how much I truly like Tim—or about the fact that I sometimes worry that he only wants to "hang out" with me (as the Earthlings say) because he is so interested in everything alien.

On the other hand, if I think about that too much, we can never be real friends.

The Fatherly One always says, "Trust, but verify." Sometimes, though, I think you just have to trust.

The Fatherly One also says that whenever two cultures meet, there are ways in which they clash. How they deal with the collision of ideas and beliefs is part of forming the relationship, and a test of a culture's maturity.

The Earthlings have so little idea of what is waiting for them out in the wider universe. But as I grow more and more fond of them, as I start to feel more at home here, I hope more and more that the Fatherly One's mission will succeed. Partly for our sake, of course; after all, it would be nice to be rich.

But even more for the sake of the Earthlings.

Do you think it will really work out for you

to visit, Maktel? I am very excited by the possibility. (If I can just keep from getting thrown off the planet before you get here. . . .)

Please write soon.

Fremmix Bleeblom!

Your pal,
Pleskit

On the following pages you will find Part Four of "Disaster on Geembol Seven"—Pleskit's story of what happened on the last planet where he lived before coming to Earth.

This story is being told in six installments, one at the end of each of the first six books of *I WAS A SIXTH GRADE ALIEN*.

The next thrilling chapter will appear in Book 5:

ZOMBIES OF THE SCIENCE FAIR

DISASTER ON GEEMBOL SEVEN

Part Four:
"City of the Constructs"

FROM: Pleskit Meenom, on Planet Earth
TO: Maktel Geebrit, on Planet Hevi-Hevi

Dear Maktel:

We now come to the difficult part of what happened on Geembol Seven.

As you will remember, I had been on the planet only a few days when the Fatherly One took me to the Moondance Celebration, where I spotted a six-eyed boy named Derrvan who clearly needed help. But it was a trap, of sorts, for when I followed him to the waterfront, I was pulled into a hidden elevator that took me (and Derrvan) down to a secret cavern.

Balteeri, the being who pulled me in, was a "construct"—an illegal combination of biological and mechanical parts. He and Derrvan wanted me to hear their story. I agreed, despite their warning that to listen was a crime. But before they could even begin, construct hunters burst through the wall of the cave. To escape we went deeper into the planet, where Balteeri had a flying ship. After a harrowing trip through rocky tunnels, we came at last to a most amazing place.

The cavern that opened below us was lit by dimly glowing spheres that floated about forty or fifty feet above its stony floor. I tried to count, but soon realized there were several hundred of the things. By their gentle light we could see that there was a small city nestled below them.

As we drew closer, I realized with horror that it was a city of constructs. That is, everyone I saw walking its streets was like Balteeri: a strange combination of natural and mechanical parts. Knowing that such creations are illegal it had been startling enough to see Balteeri. To see an entire city filled with such beings was a real *clinkus*-tightener.

Balteeri brought our ship to a gentle landing at the edge of the city. One of the glowballs floated over to hover directly above us, making it easier to walk to the city. Since the path we followed was twisty and littered with stones, I appreciated the light.

"Why have you brought me here?" I asked as we walked.

"We were being chased," snapped Balteeri. "Or have you forgotten that already?"

"How will I get back?" I asked, not caring if I sounded self-centered.

Balteeri set his jaw. "That remains to be seen."

Derrvan had said nothing since we landed. I glanced at him. He was staring ahead of us with a hungry expression, as if this was something he had been looking for, longing for, all his life. "This is my father's city," he whispered when he saw me looking at him.

"Was your father a construct?"

I asked the question timidly, not sure whether it would be offensive.

"His father was the savior of the constructs," said Balteeri grimly. "Which is what cost him his life. Now come along."

Ignoring my desire to ask more questions, he started forward. Derrvan and I followed, lagging just a few feet behind. "Do not mind Balteeri," he whispered. "He is gruff, but he has a good spirit."

Yes, but is it real or mechanical? I wondered. It was not a question I dared to ask out loud.

I had already lived on three different planets,

so I was used to being surrounded by beings who were unlike me in appearance. But never had I felt so different, so out of place, as I did in the city of the constructs, where Derrvan and I appeared to be the only beings made entirely of flesh and blood. All around us on the narrow streets were half-natural, half-mechanical creatures like Balteeri. Yet each was unique; each had his, her, or its own special combination of added parts, extra arms or legs or tails, usually with cleverly designed tools attached. Some were actually mounted on wheels and didn't walk at all. Some had most of their birth faces, with only small patches of metal or plastic; others had heads that were nearly all constructed and would have seemed robotic except for the look in their eyes.

They stared at Derrvan and me oddly as we passed. Some seemed angry, some almost hungry; some seemed to flinch at the sight of our unaltered, fully natural faces and bodies. I was struggling not to flinch myself, torn between my basic training about accepting difference and all the evil things I had heard about constructs.

"Where are we going?" asked Derrvan, after we had been walking for several minutes.

"You'll see soon enough," replied Balteeri gruffly.

Only a moment later he led us down a side street. We passed a tavern where raucous singing and laughter flowed from the open windows—an unexpected bit of warmth in this strange place. The street was quieter after that. It came to a dead end in front of a small but very beautiful building.

Without bothering to knock or ring a bell, Balteeri opened the door and stepped in. Derrvan and I followed.

"This looks like a chapel!" I exclaimed.

My surprise must have sounded in my voice, because Balteeri turned to me and said angrily, "I suppose you think that just because we're half-mechanical we have no souls."

"I hadn't thought about it at all," I said honestly. "I just wasn't expecting you to bring us to such a place."

He nodded silently, but I got the impression he found my answer acceptable. Before any of us could speak again, we heard a voice from the far end of the chapel ask, "Is someone there?" Before we could answer, the same voice cried joyfully, *"Balteeri!* You've come back. Do you have good news for us?"

Balteeri closed his eyes, and the biological half of his face looked pained. "I have but a slender thread of hope, Serha Dombalt. Nothing more."

"That is more than we have had so far," replied the *serha*, moving into the light.

Serha Dombalt wore a hooded robe of silvery blue, cinched around the waist with a black cord. The hood was up, hiding much of her face. Even so, I could see that she was a construct, not only from the glint of metallic skin that shone from beneath the robe but from the fact that one of her six-fingered hands was covered by light green flesh, while the other was made of metal and capped by fingers that each had a different mechanical design and function.

She seemed startled by the sight of Derrvan and me. "You've brought *two* organics with you," she said. In her voice I could hear curiosity, fear, and even a hint of accusation.

"This is Derrvan, whom I first went to seek," replied Balteeri. "The other is Pleskit Meenom, childling of the new ambassador from Hevi-Hevi. Derrvan and I intended only to seek his help, not bring him here. But we were pursued—"

"Are you sure you weren't followed here?" interrupted Serha Dombalt. "You could put us all in the gravest danger—"

"We are already in grave danger," replied Balteeri, his voice unexpectedly gentle. "That was the point of all this."

Serha Dombalt bowed her head. "Forgive me, Balteeri," she whispered. "It is an old reaction, and deeply ingrained."

Balteeri waved her apology aside. "The point is, as long as I have the ambassador's childling here, it makes more sense for you to tell him our story. You know it more directly than I do. Be-

sides, you're nicer than I am. The boy may be willing to hear things from you that he would resist from me."

Serha Dombalt nodded, then drew back her hood. "Come with me," she said.

Swallowing, trying to ignore the burst of fear and revulsion I felt at the sight of her half organic/half mechanical head, I walked with Derrvan and Balteeri to the front of the chapel, where Serha Dombalt led us around a speaker's stand to a narrow doorway covered by a metallic blue curtain.

We went down three steps into a small, cozy room that appeared to have been carved directly into the stone. Serha Dombalt gestured for us to sit on a long stone shelf. (Fortunately, it was covered by thick padding.)

She gazed at me intently. Her organic eye showed sorrow and compassion; her mechanical eye was cold and unblinking. "So," she said. "You are the slender vessel in which all our hopes reside."

"I do not understand! What is it you want of me?"

She closed her eyes and whispered, "We want you to save us from complete and utter destruction."

To be continued . . .

A Glossary of Alien Terms

Following are definitions for alien words and phrases that appear for the first time in this book. While most are from Hevi-Hevi, you will find a few from other alien tongues as well. (Note: definitions for alien words that first appeared in Books 1, 2, and 3 of *I WAS A SIXTH GRADE ALIEN* can be found in Books 2 and 3 of the series.)

The number after a definition indicates the chapter where the term first appears.

For most words we are only giving the spelling. In actual usage many would, of course, be accompanied by smells and/or body sounds.

ai-yi-yikkle-demonga: The literal translation of this is "Run for your life, someone's been sucking the crazy-fruit again!" However, over time it has come to be used as an all-purpose expression of fear or concern.

(Shhh-foop, by the way, is not speaking Hevi-Hevian here, but in her excitement has reverted to the language of her own world, Mirdop 2. Interestingly, "Ai-yi-yi!" as an expression of concern or fright appears in at least 419 different languages.) (15)

beezledorf: A being whose heart/head ratio is out of balance, and who therefore lets emotions rule thoughts. (Literally, a "soft thinker.") The opposite extreme is a *dartdorf*—a thought-ruled being who has forgotten the importance of emotion and feelings. (8)

bliddki: A fluffy, four-winged, birdlike creature. Often kept as a housepet on Hevi-Hevi, the *bliddki* is cherished for the sweetness of its song and the pleasing aroma of its farts. (9)

geedrill peedris fli-danji: "You are pampering these creatures!" (Not Hevi-Hevian) (12)

Kilgad-durr: Important site in Hevi-Hevian mythology; in brief, all the forces were in place for an enormous battle that would have cost tens of thousands of lives when a character called "the *sheelkirk*" (see below), beloved for her grace and beauty, made a sacrifice that so stunned the four armies involved that the battle was canceled. The moment is considered the beginning of true civilization on Hevi-Hevi. (11)

pak-skwardles: A high-protein, slightly sweet Hevi-Hevian snack made from fermented *dweezil* beans that have been stored in a cool, dark place for at least three months. (6)

pawpreet: Half of a biological unit found in the southern wampfields of Hevi-Hevi; incomplete without a *skrizzle. Pawpreets* and *skrizzles* are notorious for their stubbornness, and if they are separated, there is a fifty-fifty chance they will die before either will make a move to reconnect. It is only the ones that will overcome their tragic stubbornness that survive. (17)

serha: A being who has given its life to studying matters of the spirit; also used as a term of respect for any being considered to be particularly wise. (serial episode)

sheelkirk, the: A tragic, semidivine character in the first Hevi-Hevian epic poem; one of the most beloved characters in Hevi-Hevian mythology. (11)

skibwee: A hairy purple flower found in the northern wampfields; particularly loved for its delicate beauty and intoxicating (literally) aroma. (11)

skeegil sprixis: Literally, "Now has joy returned to me!" An all-purpose exclamation of delight coined by the poet Brigdingle the Strange. (16)

skrizzle: The dominant half of a biological unit found in the southern wampfields of Hevi-Hevi; a hard-shelled creature with a soft underbelly. (See *pawpreet*) (17)

squiboodlian: A popular stuffed toy particularly beloved by Hevi-Hevian children; by extension, a term of endearment between sweethearts. (2)

zgribnick: A word used to express distress; the equivalent of *drat* or *phooey*. (9)